Abnormal Side Effects

An Anthology

I0626776

Robert J. S. T. McCartney

A.B.Normal Publishing and Media Group™

**A.B.Normal Publishing and Media Group
PO Box 31311
Knoxville, TN 37930
www.abnormalpublishing.com**

Publisher's note: This is a work of fiction. Names, characters, places, and incidents are a product of the author's imagination. Locales and public names are sometimes used for atmospheric purposes. Any resemblance to actual people, living or dead, or to businesses, companies, events, institutions, or locales is completely coincidental.

Book Layout © 2014 BookDesignTemplates.com

Abnormal Side Effects/ **Robert J. S. T. McCartney** — First Print, 2016

To my wife, Karyn, and my kids, Zelda, and Aeris.

"There is no greater agony than bearing an untold story inside you." — **Maya Angelou**

"You must stay drunk on writing so reality cannot destroy you." — **Ray Bradbury**

"Be anything but normal."—**Robert J. S. T. McCartney**

CONTENTS

Author's Note

Good day, Reader.

I trust you are comfortable, yes? I do hope so.

Now, I am conducting a case study; a preliminary check on your psyche if you will.

I initially dubbed this project as "B-Sides." This was in contradiction to the normality (and the direct opposite) of the importance of how society views the following matters to be of little concern until it is too late. Depression, PTSD, trauma, suicide, and more. These are the abnormal side effects of life.

What follows are the tales of the many side effects millions of individuals experience daily. You will be acquainted with a few stories. Some may be more disturbing than others. Please remember that this is a work of fiction, though, the issues genuinely exist.

Life has many experiences, of which, they hold no warning labels. While most people believe themselves to be right; there exist the side effects of our existence and actions.

Do remember that life is real.

—RJM

The Crystal Manor's Secret

S IMON LOOKED OUT THE REAR WINDOW of the car as it drove up the long brick road to the grand manor. Indeed, it was a magnificent sight. It was a massive estate home built near the cliff-side overlooking a crystal-clear bay.

Gray stone laid the foundation as it stretched up towards the heavens. Gargoyles and ornate gothic rods and spikes protruded from the peaks. Wrought iron windows offered as eyes in and out of the beautiful manor where all weary travelers were welcomed to stay. As they came to a halt where an attendant gathered up their luggage, his parents began doing their usual bickering.

Simon rolled his eyes and knew that this stay was nothing that would help him, or help his parent's marriage. He had accepted that they would divorce or worst-case scenario, he'd find a place to die, and that would be it. Simon was tired of changing schools, being labeled a freak, a fat ass, and being called names, getting into fights. He was tired of being the subject of his parent's arguments and receiving persistent beatings and threats.

So many times, he had been asked how he got the bruises from, and how he got the scars on his wrists. When he was last admitted for attempting suicide, the doctors had even told his parents that they were at fault; abusive, both mentally and physically. They both replied with their typical "when and where?" snide reply.

That was a few years ago. Now, Simon was under constant supervision, given medication (which was having an adverse effect) and was forced into psychological sessions with a washed-up Broadway actor/writer that 'had a sudden change of heart.' One that had said 'so many young people are dying and are wasting their talent, and being selfish by throwing their lives away.' The egg-man always pissed him off.

He had stopped taking his medication once he noticed his suicidal tendencies were increasing and instead started self-therapy. Which began to show positive signs for himself. Save for his parents incessant probing of his affairs, reading his journal, and not helping matters he struggled with outside of the home.

His parents figured, along with the egg-man, that a family trip to the Crystal Bay Estate would benefit them all. Several thousand dollars and a 13-hour excursion, here they were.

"Time heals all wounds," he remembered someone saying. He thought it to be horse shit.

He went to the trunk of the car and motioned to carry his own case, where the attendant stopped him.

"Young sir, please allow me to get that for you." The lanky man smiled under his faux mask of obviously wanting to scream and tell the boy's parents to shut the hell up.

"No, it's quite alright. Thank you, though. Plus, you have your hands full now anyway." Simon replied, giving a slight motion of his head towards his parents.

The attendant gave a genuine smile in reply and set to loading the bags onto a trolley for the bellhop to carry in.

Simon walked towards the massive wooden doors that arched to at least 13 feet tall. The door on the right opened and gave way to a lobby that contradicted its exterior. Flesh toned and heavily induced with marble. Marble walls, marble tile, marble ceilings. So much marble! A lush red carpet stretched from the reception desk to the door, mimicking a tongue. He felt as if he was walking into a mouth more so than a lavish home remade into a hotel.

Banisters of two grand staircases on the left and right came from the second floor down to the lobby. A massive crystal chandelier hung high but sulked. Had he been several feet taller he could have probably touched it. He could make out the ornate figurines that each piece of crystal resembled. Some were horses, cows, people, birds, and other objects. It was a giant world of crystal. Transparent. Equal. And each with their unique faults.

There were magnificent elaborate tapestries that hung on the wall, further amplifying the flesh tones with its red and pink hues. Sconce lighting along some of the walls almost mimicked rows of teeth. Paintings of the founding family and its ancestors populated the walls, in line with other memorabilia and wrought iron windows that were the eyes in and out to the world. The balconies of each floor seemed to resonate an ivory tone, with spiral wrapping staircases leading to who knew where. Off on the sides were passageways labeled to the elevators, restrooms, pool house, banquet hall, kitchen, and other destinations.

Simon caught his reflection on every wall, ceiling, and floor, and it made him sick. He hated his appearance. Simon was average height for his age, and slightly overweight, though, his father would still comment that he could stand to lose 30 or so more pounds and to work out. He had short dark brown hair and brown eyes. He was pale in his facial complexion, whereas his arms and legs were a darker tone. Often, he'd be made fun of for his natural look, dubbed as a goth, freak, wannabe closet vamp, or whatever the kids thought was a hip insult today.

He shook his head and rolled his eyes. He soldiered on to the reception desk.

A short man with slick back black hair, bright blue eyes, and a crazy mustache greeted him. "Good afternoon, sir. Checking in, are we?" the man inquired professionally; his eyes seemed to exaggerate a sort of crazy. Simon liked him.

"Ah, yes, my parents and me. Last name Carroll. Nancy, Thomas, and Simon S." Simon replied.

Outside, his parents still argued with one another, while the attendant tapped the bellhop's shoulder and motioned to move the trolley indoors.

The man looked the computer screen over, "Ah here we are. You will be staying in room 318." The man rolled his r's elegantly, striking admiration in Simon. He looked back to Simon. "Ah...dear me, where are your parents?"

Simon sighed, "they're out there...still."

The man glared at the screen towards where the parents arguing began to subside finally. "Pah," the man remarked. "I apologize, young master."

Simon smiled at the crazy-eyed man, catching his name to be Sal.

"It's alright. I'm used to it," Simon sighed. "Though, I dunno if everyone here is going to want to be used to it."

The bellhop approached from behind Simon. Sal took note and motioned him over. "Please show the young master to room 318."

The bellhop nodded in compliance and ushered the man towards the elevators. As the pair of polished gray metal doors parted, he thought he heard something.

Hey. Simon looked around and didn't see anything unusual. Naturally, he shrugged it off and wandered into the elevator with the bellhop.

The bellhop was taller than Simon by a few feet. He was more well-kept than Sal, at least regarding facial hair. With a black cap strapped to his head, which seemed to camouflage his black hair. The man could have been mistaken as a floating head if anything. Black shoes, with black slacks, with black gloves, black, black, black.

"So, is your wardrobe only black or do you have a Batman cowl too?" Simon inquired.

The bellhop chuckled. "No, I have some reds too. Unfortunately, I am no Batman, though, it would be great."

Simon smiled to himself.

The bell dinged as they had arrived at the floor. The bellhop ushered Simon to the room and unloaded the trolley. Once finished, and formally introduced as Stephen, shown the quarters, where things were in the house, the Bellhop motioned his leave.

"Don't you want a tip or anything?" Simon asked.

"Normally, yes, I'd ask for a tip…but that's something your parents can afford, not you." Stephen replied.

"Well, if it's any consolation, I think I'll order room service…just put it under my dad's name and write in a suitable amount." Simon grinned.

"You're too kind, but I am afraid I must respectfully decline. I'd much rather do things the legal way…" Stephen paused, "unless they try to stiff me."

"Your secret is safe with me," Simon added.

"Good day, sir." Stephen bowed and motioned to leave the room.

"Thanks," Simon replied before Stephen exited the room, closing the door behind him.

Simon started to look around the massive room. It seemed to resemble a luxury apartment than a hotel room. There was an ornate shower enclosure, a long tub with lion claws. There was even a Jacuzzi tub in the corner that looked out to the bay below. The bathroom was nothing short of an overpriced venue of escape. There were lavish sofas, a couch, recliners, and different tables in the living area atop a plush beige carpet, with a sizeable television complete with a variety of game consoles. Pictures framed of the time spent to build the estate hung on the wall; history in pictures...history in the making. The room resonated with oodles of dollars spent on luxury and elegant living.

On the back wall, the path split into two; Simon's room was on the right, while his parent's room was on the left. He wagered a peek into his parent's bedroom but figured it was just more luxury nonsense. He strolled into his bedroom, with luggage in tow. He opened the door and thought he saw a person standing on his bed; or seemingly jumping on it. He dropped his bags and flipped on the light, causing the anomaly to vanish.

Maybe it's just me being tired. It was a hell of a trip after all.

He grumbled to himself something incoherently.

His room mirrored the same lavish style that was portrayed in the living room. Except he had his own blissful view of Crystal Bay. He placed his bags down by his bed and stood by the window. He took in the fantastic sight of the bay and the cliff that jutted out towards the bay. He swore he could see a kid sitting on the ledge. He blinked, and then it was gone.

He drew the shade and the curtains and wagered to get some sleep. He turned around and caught earshot of his parents coming to the room; still bickering. He let out a sigh and closed his room's door in time as they entered.

He plopped down on the soft bed and rolled over to his left. He knew his parents were coming to check on him.

"Simon? Are you in here?" his mother inquired as she peeked in his room.

"Nope. Just some guy," Simon replied.

His mother rolled her eyes. "Well, if some guy would like dinner, I recommend getting it now. We have an early start tomorrow morning. Or do you want to waste it all by sleeping in?"

"I don't know. Do you want to waste it all by arguing with dad?" he countered.

"Don't get smart with me, young man!" his mother raised her voice and threw open the door.

"Nancy, don't take it out on him. He's right. Let's take a breath. Calm down." Simon heard his dad trying to gather his mother.

Simon grinned at the attempt his father was making at controlling his temper.

Nancy stomped her foot. "I am calm! Don't tell me to be calm! I am calm Goddammit!" Nancy retaliated back.

"No, you're not. You're causing a ruckus on night one of our retreat…and you're only going to make matters worse," Thomas coolly replied.

Nancy flipped the light switch off and pulled the door shut with force. "Oh, so he gets a pass at being depressed and angry because he's a spoiled little shit? 'Oh, woe is me. My life is so difficult,'" she mockingly whined.

Simon and Thomas both sighed at the same time through separate rooms. A common formality both father and son shared.

"And you wonder why he's tried to kill himself? He's going through a tough time…" Thomas mumbled.

"A tough time? TOUGH TIME?! A tough time was when I was raped by your so-called 'best friend.' And what did you do? You did nothing! Just be thankful that Simon is your son because I would have killed him and that son of a bitch myself." Nancy raged on.

"Stop it. STOP IT!" Thomas yelled back, his patience becoming lost.

Simon started to drown out the yelling. It was nothing different. Though, he supposed it was a reasonable way to fall asleep. To drift off to the world of nothingness…the sea of the eternal void. Occasionally, he'd have a dream here or there. He loved them, even if they would be torturous or be something so horrible. It was better than dreaming of nothing.

As he fell asleep, he could feel as if there was something…or someone watching him. He could feel a hint of sadness emanate nearby. From something…someone.

He rolled over and brought his arms and legs in and silently rocked to sleep.

****

He awoke the next day with the sun piercing through the curtains and shade. He let out a yawn that ached his jaw and cracked his back. Truth be told, it was the best sleep he ever had. He had a magnificent dream too. He dreamt that other kids surrounded him, both younger and older than he and that they were all having fun playing with one another. He felt no pain, no anger, no resentment. He felt nothing but pure joy and happiness.

He hopped out of bed with renewed vigor and changed his attire for the day. He figured he'd go simple, a black polo, black slacks, and his black shoes. To everyone else, it was his undertaker attire. To him, it was life.

He went over to the window and looked out. The view with the sun high in the sky was a spectacular spectacle. The water shimmered like diamonds passing by one another. The blue of the sky radiated; magnified a thousand-fold by the surface of the bay. The bay mirrored the heavens flawlessly. He could see why it was dubbed Crystal Bay.

He went to the bathroom, having already taken note that his parents had left him. He ventured out to the living area and found a note on the coffee table.

He mumbled as he read it aloud. "Gone to breakfast and then for a walk with your mother. Go help yourself to whatever you want. Love Dad."

Simon rolled his eyes and scoffed at the note. He then shrugged it off. He was feeling good; the best he had felt in a long time, and he wasn't going to let a simple note or last night's shenanigans ruin it for him.

Simon walked down the hall, retracing his steps back to the lobby. As he meandered through the halls, he could feel sudden and ominous spots. Like he wasn't the only one in the hallway. He turned around and looked down the hallway, thinking he caught the sound of a child laughing down the hallway. Nothing.

Shrugging it off as nothing, Simon continued his journey to downstairs for some morning grub. He gave a wave to Stephen and Sal at the reception desk. Both gave a wave and nod back.

As Simon rounded the corner to the hallway that led to the kitchen and dining room, he caught a girl that seemed to be around the same age as him that almost leveled him. She was petite, with long brown hair, emerald eyes, milky skin, and dressed in kitchen attire: a food-stained white button-down shirt, black slacks, and black shoes.

"Woah!" Simon caught the girl.

"Oh, I am so sorry. Excuse me," the girl said.

Simon chuckled, "it's quite alright."

The two tried to evade each other's path but ended up only blocking one another. Each smiling and laughing at the ordeal.

Simon stood and waved her by, smiling.

The girl smiled as she passed by, looking behind at him as she was then out of view.

Simon smiled to himself and sighed.

He finally got to the kitchen and dining room. The dining room was massive and had a marbled stone from ceiling to floor. Giant crystal chandeliers hung low from the vaulted ceiling that was painted with a mural of a bunch of angels and children playing in heaven. The lights were draped with crimson silk drapes stretching from one to the other. Elegant tapestries, flags, and other wall décor hung on the walls. There were small pedestals of plants, vases, sculptures, suits of armor. A massive, sprawling dark rug stretched out to the entire length and width of the rooms' colossal cherry table. Smaller tables and chairs were sporadically and strategically placed around.

He gazed around for a hint of his mother and father and found they were not here. To this, he smiled wildly.

As he wandered out towards an empty table, a young woman came over and greeted him with a bright smile. "Hello, sir. Will you be dining with us this morning?"

Simon glanced at the woman's name tag that prominently read Brandi. She was petite, with shoulder-length brown-black hair tightly wound up in a bun. Her facial features, stature, and slightly darkened skin tone suggested she was of Native American descent. Her eyes a green-brown, with ruby red lipstick. To him, she was quite attractive, even if she was quite older than him. She wore the same attire all the other female servers wore: black slacks, black pumps, a black server apron, with a white button-down blouse.

"Yes, ma'am," Simon replied.

"This way please," Brandi said as she escorted Simon to his seat.

Simon sat down and gave another look at the room that seemed to engulf him. "It's quite an impressive view," he said.

"Yes, it never seems to get old," she said looking at the fantastic room they stood in.

Brandi handed Simon a menu and inquired his preference of beverage. Before long, she came back with a drink in hand, and ready to take his order.

After rattling off his order, Simon continued to stare in awe at the masterful room. He took note of several other guests that sat around. Some were happy, some sad. He took note of one couple that together. An older couple, much like his mother and father. The man ate his breakfast, while the woman picked at it, her head heavy in her hand. He watched her for a moment as he took a sip of his orange juice, then she started to cry hysterically. The man waved over a waiter and said a few words, before going around the table and escorting his wife out of the dining room.

He shrugged it off as nothing of importance…however, he had a nagging feeling that he couldn't quite shake from it. As he looked around again, he took note of some of the couples. Most were childless or had older children. To him, he found it strange.

****

Breakfast had passed, and Brandi came back with the bill.

He wrote a note with a joke on it and gave the room information, with a generous tip. He started to leave when he looked up and thought he saw a little boy swinging from the chandelier. He fell back, startled at the sight. Others looked at him as if he was crazy. He looked back up only to see nothing there. The chandelier, however, was still moving slightly.

A few of the staff started to come over, but he waved them off, signaling that he was OK. He dusted himself off and sighed. Believing he saw things and that he just made himself look like a fool.

Simon figured he'd wager a venture outside to view the property. One of his stops being the overlook that he saw from his room. As Simon wandered through the halls to the lobby, he overheard a conversation he wasn't happy to have stumbled upon.

"That's the tenth case this year," Sal stated as he wiped his brow with a white handkerchief.

"Let's just hope that there aren't any more freak accidents or kids that go missing. I don't know how much more I can take, with parents finding their child dead or having them go missing while on vacation," another employee said quietly.

Dead and missing children? What? Simon thought, confused.

He looked outside through the open doors and saw an ambulance escorting a gurney with a white sheet over it. Curiosity took the reins. "What happened?" he asked.

"Oh, dear me," Sal jumped, startled, "ho, you gave me quite the scare."

"I apologize," Simon replied. "Would you care to tell me what happened though?"

The employees looked to one another. One of the bellhops looked at Sal and waved 'goodbye.' The other bellhop left in haste. Eventually, they all left Sal alone with the young inquiring individual.

"Ah, well, you see, young master," Sal hesitated. "I am not at liberty to discuss private matters you're not privy to."

Simon nodded. "I understand."

A deep voice behind Simon caused him to jump. "Dead…"

Simon turned around to the man he saw earlier at the table with his wife, who had the breakdown. His face was red—flushed. His eyes pink and his person as messy as it was when he last saw him. He could tell that the man usually kept himself tidy and clean—which was comparable to how he saw the man before him now.

"Our boy died this morning." The man seemed to reek of liquor and alcohol as he slurred the sentence.

"I am sorry for your loss," Simon replied, saddened by the unfortunate piecing of the morning's puzzle.

"I heard him jumping on his bed. He was laughing…and was as if he was talking to someone else in the room. The next thing we knew, we heard a thud. We didn't think anything of it at first." The man rubbed his face and his hair back. Trying to control his emotions. "Then—then I went in to check on him because we were going to have breakfast. He was—he was just lying there…on the floor." The man then lost it and started to sob uncontrollably. "I'm sorry, I'm so sorry."

Sal came around the desk and ushered the man to another room to calm down.

Simon watched the men disappear into the room together. He could hear the sobbing of the man get more frequent and reach hysterical levels. He couldn't help but feel sad for the man and woman.

He looked towards the doors as they started to close and the ambulance began its departure.

****

Simon wandered around outside, walking close to the edge of the cliff that gave way to the rocky bottom and shoreline. He watched the tide gently roll in and go back out. He had finally made it to the overlook. He sat down and looked at the backside of the manor and the shimmering bay. He saw boats parading around the inlet, some close enough that he could still make the delicate features. He remembered when he wasn't arguing with his father or being lectured, that they used to love watching boats together. A fond memory he kept. One of the few he treasured. There were a few good memories of his mother, but after he found out about the rape and the diagnosis.

Simon shook his head. However, wasn't the time to dwell on things that were not in his capable hands. This trip was to be one better himself…and hopefully, his parents better themselves.

As he looked out, he felt a presence next to him. He looked over and saw a boy much younger than him, sit next to him. He was a short, with blond hair, eyes like the sky, and very pale.

He wore some argyle sweater and dark slacks, and black dress shoes. He watched Simon closely.

"Hi," said Simon.

The boy continued to stare at him.

"What's your name?" Simon asked looking over at the boy.

"Robin," replied the boy.

Simon returned his gaze back to the bay. "Do you come here often?" Simon asked.

"Sometimes. I like it." Robin then looked out at the bay. "It's pretty, isn't it?"

Simon nodded. "It sure is."

"What's your name?" Robin asked.

"Simon."

"How old are you?"

"14. I'll be 15 next month," Simon replied.

Robin began kicking his feet in and out against the cliff. "That's cool."

"Are you staying here?" Simon inquired.

"I live here," Robin replied.

"Oh yeah? That's gotta be pretty cool. To have that big of a house and all this." Simon added.

"Yeah. I used to be lonely, but I've made friends with the kids that come and go," Robin said, giving a slight chill to his words.

"Yeah, I hear ya," Simon sighed. "I get called names, made fun of, get into fights, bad situation with my parents." Simon shook his head.

"Why don't you leave?" Robin asked.

"Well, I can't exactly just up and leave. I have responsibilities," Simon replied.

"If your parents lash out at you, blame you, beat you; while others call you names, pick on you and callously disregard you…why bother staying around?" said Robin.

Simon chuckled. "Are you sure you're not older?" he scanned the bay lazily. His depression starting to gnaw at him. "You seem to know me quite well, Robin."

"I know what it was like," said Robin. "Then one day, I vowed that I wouldn't take it anymore. So, I came here."

"Away from your family?" Simon asked.

Robin nodded. "Yep. Now I live here. I can have fun as much as I want, no one makes fun of me, no one gives me hell for staying up late, and no one can hurt me."

Another chill went down Simon's back. "Well, I'm glad to see things worked out good for you, Robin."

Robin nodded and gave a sly grin. He sighed and bit his lower lip. "The only problem is, is it gets cold in the house. Especially, at night."

"Have you tried raising the temperature in your room?" Simon asked.

Robin shook his head. "It's OK, it's just something I have yet to get used to."

"I'm sorry to hear that," Simon apologized. He looked up at the sun and wagered that his parents probably would want to do something as a family. "Well, I hate to cut it short, but I have to get back. My folks might be looking for me."

Robin nodded. "Good luck, Simon. I'll be around…"

The voice seemed to trail off. For as Simon looked back as he made his way down the path, Robin was gone.

****

Simon made his way back to the manor and saw Stephen, sitting in the lobby with his hat in his hands.

"Hey, Stephen."

"Oh, hey—I'm sorry, what was it again? Simon?" Stephen fumbled with his memory of the young man.

"Yeah." Simon smiled. "Hey, by chance, did you get a good tip from my parents?"

"Yeah, your father gave a generous tip. I appreciate the thought." Stephen gave a light chuckle.

Simon sat down near the on-break bellhop. Then Simon asked the nagging question that had been on his mind since overhearing the conversation of earlier and with Robin. "Hey, do you know of the kid that died this morning?"

Stephen went blank. He looked around the lobby, at the reception desk, everywhere. "I can't really tell you…"

"Oh, that's OK, I understand. I was just curious." Simon replied smiling.

Stephen leaned in close to Simon, whispering. "Ever since the youngest boy of the estate died, there has been creepy happenings all throughout the house."

"How long ago was that?" Simon whispered.

"More than a hundred or so years ago," Stephen replied.

"What was his name by chance?" Simon asked.

Sal called for Stephen. "Stephen, I need your help for a moment."

"Sorry, I have to go." Stephen rushed off to the reception desk, donning his hat.

Simon mulled over the possibility that perhaps… No, that couldn't be right. He seemed alive. Besides…

"There's our boy." Thomas strolled in with Nancy holding his hand. "How are you doing, kiddo?"

"Hey mom, dad… I'm doing alright," Simon replied.

"Good. Did you sleep well?" Thomas inquired.

"Yeah with all things considered," Simon replied and then immediately apologized after finishing his sentence.

"It's alright, son. Your mother and I are the ones that should be saying we're sorry," Thomas said.

A throbbing pain began to surge in his head, causing him to fall to his knees. He clenched his head and started to groan in pain.

"Son, Simon, are you alright?" Thomas' voice seemed to echo.

The room spun around and soon faded to black.

****

Simon woke up and found himself in bed. The day was dark, and the place only donned in black. His right eye and cheek felt swollen. He ran his hand over his cheek and winced in pain. His right eye gave some difficulty in seeing things.

He wondered what the hell had happened, and then he remembered. After saying his remark, he was decked with a left and then a right, and was sent head first to the ground.

Go figure, he thought.

He sighed as he sat up. He thought of Robin, of the boy that had died. The boy's parents…how they cared so much about their son.

At least he had folks that gave a damn and grieved for him.

Then he thought of the girl he ran into in the hallway. He had hoped to see her again. If anything, he needed to see her again.

****

Simon got out of bed and dressed. His parents weren't in the room, still, something he was accustomed to. He ventured out into the hallway and began to set off for something to eat. As he strolled, he felt the familiar hot and cold sensations that would occasionally pass through him. He kept going, though. He wanted to see if he could find that girl again. Even if by chance.

He took a more direct route to the dining hall and kitchen. Sure enough, he saw the girl working in the kitchen. She was still as cute as he remembered her. He felt as if his heart skipped a few beats at the sight of her.

He started to wander to the dining hall when he heard a commotion going on in the kitchen. He hurried back to see a crowd of people looking in a shaft. Curious, he wandered into the kitchen.

"What's going on?" he asked.

"Sophie's stuck in there," an elderly woman in apron and hairnet replied.

"Well, maybe I can help?" Simon stated.

"Don't be silly, you'll probably get stuck in there too!" The woman scoffed at Simon's offer.

Simon sensed an urgency and gambled on the whim. "Well, I guess we'll find out."

He rushed for the shaft and began meandering through it. "What the hell was she doing in here?" he asked aloud as he crawled.

Not far off in it, he found Sophie stuck. Her butt in his direction. "Uh, ahem," he cleared his throat.

"Is somebody there?" the girl replied panicked.

"Yes, uh, I am, uh…behind you," Simon replied, blushing.

"Can you help me, please?" Sophie grunted trying to get unstuck.

"Yeah, let me see." Simon approached her and began assessing the situation.

"Is it OK if I try to maneuver you, so you get unstuck?" Simon asked.

"What? What kind of question is that? Of course!" Sophie slammed her palms down on the shaft that trapped her.

"You know...people...society nowadays," Simon grumbled.

He began trying to maneuver her hips, legs, and feet. "You're pant leg is stuck. I'm going to try and rip at the seam, alright?"

"Wouldn't it just be easier then to take my pants off?" Sophie replied.

Simon felt his face turning red. "Uh, I don't think that'd be necessary."

He tugged on the fabric and tried to tear it. Finally, it gave way, letting the girl's leg free, and caused a kick to Simon's head.

Something else also gave way in that shaft. Accidentally or intentionally, all according to one's plan...something. Simon and Sophie fell into an abandoned room.

The pair coughed and dusted off.

"Are you alright?" Simon asked, helping Sophie up to her feet.

"Yeah, I'm fine," she replied, looking at her rescuer. "I know you, from yesterday, right?"

Simon nodded, "Yeah. I'm Simon."

"Sophie," she smiled. "Well, thanks for helping me."

Simon chuckled. "Well, I don't know if it was of much help. I mean...the state of things we're in now."

There was very little light in the room. It was nothing but old gray bedrock that smelled of must and of an age that had since long past. On one wall, there was a small door, one that no one no bigger than a child could go through.

Simon felt drawn to this door as if being told to go to it and open it.

"What is that?" Sophie asked.

"Let's find out," said Simon as he walked over to the small door.

Sophie looked around the dark room. "This place gives me the creeps."

In the shaft, debris could still be heard falling, while voices called for the pair that now wandered into foreign territory.

Simon crouched down and reached for the small wooden door. He opened it and found a little tunnel. He fumbled around in his pockets and pulled out his cellphone. He switched on the light and scanned around. Both behind him and in the shaft.

"How about you stay here, and I'll look?" Simon asked Sophie.

"Oh, hell no, I am not going to stay here in the dark. I've seen enough horror movies."

Simon laughed genuinely. A warm feeling overcame him while in the presence with Sophie.

Slowly, the pair began to investigate the tunnel. A horrible smell would strike at the pairs' senses ever so often.

"Ugh, what died down here?" Sophie asked.

After some time of crawling, Simon asked, "Where do you think this goes?"

"I have no idea. I just started here a few months ago," Sophie replied.

"Did you hear about the boy who died this morning?" Simon inquired.

"Yeah, sad," Sophie replied empathetically.

They came across various toys in the tunnel: a red tricycle, a round leather ball, a wooden horse…

Then they came across a skeleton. One was in the fetus position on the floor.

"Oh my God, oh my God," Sophie clung to Simon. "Is that—is that a skeleton?

"Yeah, it looks like it." Simon examined the remains. "Looks like a child."

"What the hell happened in here?" Sophie asked.

Simon's phone flickered on and off. He smacked it against his palm. The light came back on and he shined it in front of his path. In front of him was a decrepit little boy that was enraged at the sight. He hissed and snarled at the pair.

"What are you doing here?!" the boy yelled.

"I was just trying to help her out, and we fell," Simon panicked in his reply. "We don't mean you any harm."

The boy then gained composure and smiled at Simon. "I got you good," It laughed.

Simon stared confused. "Wait…Robin?"

"Ah, you got me," he giggled. "Or should have I gone, 'boo!'?"

"You…you're a ghost?" Simon was dumbfounded.

"Yeah. I have been for a while." Robin sighed. He pointed at the skeleton on the ground, "That's me."

"What happened?" Simon asked.

"Well, remember I said I had run away? I had found the room when they were building. I used to come in here to play by myself. To get away from others—my family." Robin sighed. "I don't remember much, but my dad had found me and began to beat me. I only remember waking up and trying to leave. Unfortunately, the was door sealed, and the room at the end of the hall was sealed off." He shrugged at the two, "My family's dark secret. Congratulations, you two know it now."

"That's horrible," Simon and Sophie both said.

"I grew lonely over the years…but other kids began to notice me. Those who were neglected, beaten, had a void in their life. So, I began making friends. I'd often ask them if they'd want to join me in having fun forever." Robin looked down at the ground, then back at Simon and Sophie.

"So, the kids that have died over the years…is because of you?" Simon asked.

"Yes…and no," Robin replied. "I never forced anyone to stay here. I never killed anyone, or hurt anyone. I only freed them—gave them a choice. I was there when they'd make their choice. When all hope was lost, when everything in life seemed to be stacked against them. When no one else noticed them, I was the one that was there to guide them."

"Robin, you know there were…there are a lot of sad parents, though, right?" Simon said.

"I do, and I feel bad. I only wanted other kids to be happy. I thought giving them release would be the way." Robin then sighed. "You understand what it's like, don't you, Simon?"

Simon nodded. "I do. However, there is always another way." He looked back at Sophie.

Robin looked to Sophie. "Are you enjoying yourself here?" he asked.

"W—what do you mean?" Sophie replied.

"You've been alone for some time. You—" Sophie cut Robin off.

"You don't know who I am or what I've been through."

Simon felt sad for Sophie. He knew she was withholding a lot. "Sophie, c'mon, let's get out of here."

"Robin, can you help us out of here?" Simon asked.

"Sure." Robin flickered as a manifestation and then vanished. He then passed through the two teenagers.

Cold shivers ran down their spines, as they started to turn back.

Once they were back in the room, Robin pointed at the shaft above them. "That's your ticket out."

"We can't reach that." Said Simon.

"Use your phone and call for help. The staff should have done so already, but with help like nowadays, who knows. No offense, Sophie." Said Robin.

"I'll come back for you, Robin." Said Simon.

"Sort yourselves out. We're all fine here." Robin replied.

Then, other children, of all ages, sizes, and genders came into the room.

Sophie gasped at the sight of all the departed children, "My God, there are so many."

Robin smiled at the pair. "Remember, you're always welcome to stay with us, should you ever want to."

****

Soon enough, the phantoms all vanished. Simon then tried calling the reception desk to try and get help. After a while, rescue crews came and got Simon and Sophie out. Investigators found the remains of Robin Cornelius Crystal Jr.

As it was a family tradition, he was to be buried in the estates' cemetery. Simon was greeted by his parents. The thought that perhaps his parents would be happy to see him, that maybe they missed him, that maybe, just maybe…they cared that he was down in a hole, with no hopes of seeing the lights of day. It was all for naught.

They had dragged him back to their room and scolded him. Slapping him upside the head, across the mouth. Pushed him against the wall, kicked him when he was down. His father's new method and attempts of trying patience were all gone. He unleashed Hell upon his son, with his mother in hot pursuit. While he was getting pelted by slaps, fists full of anger, and kicks to the gut, he thought of Robin. He also thought of the time, although it was brief, with Sophie.

After the beating had ended. Simon overheard his mother on the phone with his psychiatrist. She called him a sham, and that he had ripped them off; that this 'family' trip was a farce. The medication he suggested for Simon had no effect. As he laid on the floor and listened to his parents argue over divorce and hurled more insults at one another, a voice came to him.

Remember, you're always welcome to stay with us, should you ever want to.

"Robin..." Simon called out.

Nothing.

"Robin...will you help me?" Simon asked aloud.

He heard his parents take note of him talking to himself. Both exchanged insults over who he inherited being crazy from. Then there was the notion that his mother wasn't raped, but in fact, had cheated on his father with his best friend. His father disregarded it and said he slept with her best friend in retaliation, that he already knew the truth. That the tumor diagnosis was all a ruse to gain sympathy and she had secretly bribed a doctor.

The voices, slapping...everything drowned out to nothing.

"I'm here, Simon," said Robin. "We're all here."

Robin and the other kids all began to appear, coming through the walls. All staring at the battered teenager on the floor.

Simon reached to his feet and opened the window. He looked out to the bay. "Does it—will it hurt?"

"Only for a moment. After that, you will no longer feel any pain," said Robin.

Simon stepped up onto the ledge and sat down on it. He began thinking about Sophie. "She's the only one that may actually miss me."

Robin replied, "No, she won't."

Simon dropped his head.

"Because I'm here too..." said Sophie as she appeared coming through the wall.

He smiled as he saw her, and felt saddened that she had died too.

"It was my choice, Simon. Just as it is yours. We're all with you. We can all be together and be here. Forever." Sophie said as she walked over and caressed his cheek. A cold shiver ran down his spine.

"What the hell was that?" Simon heard his parents turn their attention to his room.

Thomas and Nancy threw open the door. All the hate, all the shame, the mistrust…everything…went out the window. Their hearts heavy—they both choked at the sight that befell them.

"Simon, no—no, please, don't," they pleaded.

"You only care about yourselves, your money. You never cared about me. Not even when I was a baby. You have hated me since day one," Simon said, the words biting harshly. Thomas tried to take a step forward. "No! Don't, don't even try, because I will go."

"Simon, please, son, we're sorry. We're just going through a tough time," Thomas pleaded.

"A tough time, huh? I've been nothing but a tough time for you both. I was nothing but a mistake. A costly mistake. I am tired—so, so tired of the beatings, being called names; by you and all the kids at school. Being made fun of, telling me that I am fat. Laughing and making a mockery of my suicide attempts. Why aren't you saying 'Do it! Do it now you son of a bitch!' huh?"

Thomas slowly took a step towards Simon. "Simon, I know you're in pain...I am sorry. I—I don't know what came over me. I want to make things right."

"Don't you do it, Simon. Don't you fucking do it!" Nancy shouted hysterically.

"Funny. You suddenly now care. No more tax credit. No more leeching. Just think though, no more bills. No more debt because of me. Now you can work, party, lie, cheat, steal from each other, and despise one another without me to be in the middle." Simon began to start crying. "All I ever wanted...was to be loved by you. For you to be there for me. To stick up for me."

"We hear you, Simon. Come down from there, and we'll help you." Thomas said as he inched closer.

"No!" Simon snapped back. "I know you. You think you know me, but I—I know you. That's why...that's why I am going on my terms and by my own free will." Simon then let go of the window sill and ledge.

"No, Simon!" Both parents screamed. Thomas dove for his son, grazing his backside. Feeling him slip through his fingertips.

Simon fell from up high and landed upon the rocky shoreline of Crystal Bay, far beneath the manor. He later awoke and found himself wandering the estate. He walked up to the cliff that jutted out into the bay, where he first met Robin. Here he saw Robin sitting. He sat down next to him. Sophie came over and sat down next to him as well. She put her hand in his, while the three of them stared on at the boats that sailed in the bay.

****

While authorities carried out the bodies of Sophie and Simon, the other kids that had died played throughout the house. Some rode banisters down or swung from the chandeliers.

After a time spent at the manor, Simon took notice that some of the kids would disappear for a little while. Robin said they'd often pay visits to their parents from time to time. Simon wagered he could pay his parents a visit but decided against it. That he'd rather stay here at the manor, with Sophie at his side, watching the boats and other kids.

The Crucifixion of Edward Croix

"THERE ARE WORSE THINGS in life than death." It's true, at least for me anyway. I don't even know how long it's been. I've lost count of the days and stopped caring really. There's no hope of leaving this place; truth be told, alive or dead, and in all honesty, I'd say preferably the latter.

My name is Edward Croix. I used to be a pawn in the vast game called Wall Street. I was married, had kids, had a lovely house with a white picket fence…I can hardly remember much of my past life before being taken. All I know is, I had it all, I wanted more, and that led to me being here.

There is little to no light in here. I can't see my hands, hell, I can't even tell if my eyes are open. All around me, the darkness plays its tricks on me, but the shadows are my only company. I have no real clothing on, save for my underwear…if there was much of that left. It's probably more like a loin cloth now, I guess. There are no nearby lakes, bodies of water. No railways, highways, or other things to distinguish exactly where the hell I am. It's just cold and dark.

Yes, I'd rather be elsewhere, anywhere in fact, but here even in a grave. You may be wondering where I am? What kind of predicament am I in? I honestly haven't an answer that could make sense; other than that, I believe Hell could be a lot more of a lovely retreat than where I am. There are screams all around me from people. I can hear kids crying, screaming. There's blood dripping off the equipment they use to torture folks. They even have animals; dogs, cats, and God only knows what else to fuel their sick, demented wheel of torment.

At times, I suppose it'd be night? Well, at night time, they gather up the 'lucky few'—as they call them—and moments later you can hear these heinous and atrocious whirling sounds—like a blender, or a grinder. I'd press my face up against the cold metal door, trying to peek in the small sliver of a crack, down the hall at the ever-so-warm light at the end of the corridor. For a moment, you hear them all clamoring, screaming, begging for their lives, and then a few seconds later—nothing. Nothing but soggy meat sloshing around. To which, I suppose that's probably what they feed us. Typically, I can hear someone whistling a tune while he makes the makeshift meatloaf. It's catchy really. Sometimes I feel tempted to whistle along with, but I guess that would be immoral.

I have no cellmate. No one to converse with over our shared fate. They like us weak. In fact, they prefer to break our ankles, our feet, our kneecaps—and for good measure, cut our Achilles' tendon. You eventually become accustomed to crawling around. Once, someone tried to strangle one of the guys when they brought food. Props to them...they killed one of the bastards, but they got a one-way ticket to the chef's choice platter. From what I could hear, they strung the guy up; limb by limb gave him a saline bag and started dismembering him piece by piece. Each time, they'd cauterize the wounds. The guy had a hell of a will to live, I'll say.

Eventually, they severed his genitals and his tongue...and well...had fun with his orifices using said items. I'd like to think he passed before then, but I don't know. They probably had fun further defecating, desecrating and fornicating with the poor saps dismembered body.

You'd think that being kept in the dark; you'd not be able to picture things so vividly. However, you hear things, smell things—God, do you smell things, taste things...and you can see clearly in the night; the things that go more than "bump in the night." You never get a look at their faces. You never see anyone's face—not even your own. Well, I suppose that's not entirely true. There was a guy named Keith, good guy, I guess. Well, he had an unfortunate run-in with one of the guys. Apparently, there was an exchange of some sexual favors and well...one of the supers caught wind of things and didn't like the idea of one of the guys spoiling the goods for The Boss. Seeing as he loved his keep fresh, and somewhat clean—least of STDs. Well, old Keith and the one guy had a face swap. The Doc, as he was called, came in and had a field day. He took a box cutter and made Keith's face come off, and swapped it with the one guy's. I'd say it was a good several hours of screaming. I didn't get sleep that night. Last, I remembered, they wanted to have some more fun with their bodies, but The Boss got tired of it all and ordered them to be tossed into the burn pit.

The women were treated the worst here. Most were slaves: either for sex, 'housework,' more sex, entertainment [did I mention sex?], and the cruel bearing of The Boss' bastard children. It didn't matter to them if they were fat, skinny, big titted, big assed, small and tight, tiny, tall. They were all meat...for pleasure and nourishment. Rape was, of course, standard. They'd have massive orgies in The Boss' lair, dinner parties...I'm using 'dinner' lightly here. They'd have wrestling matches, stripteases, and other typical outside events; just with a slight twist where the loser would be devoured by either animals, ghouls—which was a horrible fate in itself, or be dragged to the chef to do as he pleased.

The children...Mother of God...the things they'd make the children do, participate in, brainwash them to become...I get so furious! If there were anything worthwhile in here for me to do, it'd be to slay all these bastards and at the very least, free the kids. They make them perform heinous acts, lewd and crude. They rape them. They make brothers and sisters copulate against their will, and join them. If I ever can get out of here, I will make them all pay!

What's the use? All the anger I possess, all the seething hatred I have for this place, and the last small sliver of the will to live I own is nothing. I am nothing. I should just kill myself. No…no, I can't do that. I've tried a few times, but they always have a way to revive you. I guess I just wasn't trying hard enough.

Days pass like water, and still, here I am. Locked up. Hungry. Alone. Furious. Depressed. Hell-bent. Murderous. I've had some dreams as of late. Ones where I walk again, fleet-footed in fact. I tear open and spill the blood of my captors, and free the oppressed. It's a glorious dream. Sometimes, I have visions of my past life: kids, wife, all the good times. I miss my kids. I miss my wife. I don't even know if they're alive anymore. Once, they had tried to break me by torturing and killing a woman, and two kids in front of me. I knew it wasn't them. I knew they were coaxed into screaming my name and saying "Daddy!" I am anything but stupid. Though, still, I felt sorry for the women and children, and their broken family. However, I wasn't going to be broken. It had been some time since then. I forget how much time had passed. I think it was six months or a year now. I'll admit I cried for them, but not the way they wanted me to, but because of the loss of innocence.

Someone's coming! Heavy footsteps…It's The Boss! The Boss was a giant of a man, at least, his shadow was. It's always so dark…so, so very dark. His voice was deep and raspy;

sounded like he was from the Deep South. I could faintly see his Cheshire smile, "Let's get you out, stretch your legs a bit."

I looked about and saw two shadows of men come into my cell and motion for me. I just sat there. I didn't care. However, I was intrigued as to what my fate would become. They drug me down the corridor, towards that lovely glow…and here I was beginning to think it was my end. Voices whispered, heavy breathing from rooms here and there. Some cried, some laughed. It was a madhouse.

They brought me to a stone room where a large wrought iron brazier flickered wildly in the center. The fluorescent lights from above hurt my eyes something fierce. The sat me down on a wooden bench. Comfortable, I thought. There were stretching boards, makeshift crosses, bloody barrels, an iron maiden, and countless other torture paraphernalia. On a solid oak bloodstained table, there was a bone saw, pliers, crowbar, baseball bat, drills, needles, a handgun. A handgun! I couldn't take my eyes off that instrument of salvation. I glanced at it only momentarily, noting its presence, and my brilliant mind began imagining the way to break free.

The Boss was an older white fellow, long black matted hair, and goatee. He was relatively fit, at least in the arms. He had a big gut that protruded under his dingy white t-shirt. He wiped his hands on his bloodstained blue jeans, further adding to the makeshift paint job. He knelt before me, peering at me with his icy blue eyes—the flames flickering fiercely to match his crazy. "Do you know why you're here?"

I cocked my head slightly, pondering, and seemingly being the smart ass, I was. "No, sir, but it's something that I've always wanted to know since you placed me in this hell hole. Would you mind enlightening me?"

The Boss smiled an ice cream smile. "You got a smart mouth there, boy. You know what'll happen if you run it too much, right?"

I shrugged, "Well, shucks, Boss, ya got me there! I reckon you'd string me up and fuck me in the ass with a two-by-four, and then throw me on the fire rack, or some shit!"

The Boss and the guys had a laugh. I'll admit it; I did too. "Well, well, you're still quite the firecracker, even after all this time. I'll tell you what. You can keep your tongue..." The Boss motioned towards me, reaching behind and pulling out a Bowie knife. "But I am going to take one of your fingers. Do you know what I am going to do with that finger?"

"Guessing shove it up your ass, and either force feed it to me, or shove it up my ass, or some dosey doe, Cotton-eyed Joe." I instantly followed up. I didn't care. There was nothing they could do to me that could break me. Not anymore.

"Ha ha, hmm. Yes, sir, you're a tough one." The Boss sneered, "I wonder, though, if you'll be so tough," he stood up and motioned for his lackeys, "when I start your fire."

One of the guys handed The Boss a gas can. He doused me with the entire contents and then struck a match. "Any last words, boy?"

I smiled, proudly, profoundly. "I'll see you in Hell, you son of a bitch."

"Fair enough," he replied.

At that moment, as that match fell to meet with me, igniting my fiery fate. I knew whatever strength I possessed left, whatever will there was…I had to make this chance, this final attack count. I had to make good on my premise. The gun was still within reach, and though my legs were crippled and mangled, I had grown accustomed to being nimble on them. I sprung from the bench made my move—going for the handgun. The match fell and ignited the bench; with the trail of fire leaping in hot pursuit. The guys slowly motioned to interrupt my efforts, as did The Boss. In fact, he was able to get a good stab in my side, but that wasn't good enough to save him…any of them. I grabbed my instrument of retribution, and fired several shots at the guys and The Boss; each had three in the gut, and a lovely hole between the eyes.

The flames had caught up by now. Burnt flesh smells horrible as does burnt hair. Albeit, I'd rather the smell any day than the incredible amount of pain it sent me into. There was one thing I was thankful for; I always had a plan. You see, when I came into the room, I spotted a trough with water. They guys liked to do the whole…waterboarding, CIA type thing, dunk people, etc. In a fiery bolt, I dashed and plummeted into that vat of relief. It still hurt like hell (putting it mildly), but it was better than being on fire. When I got out of the trough, the pain had remained consistent, but adrenaline was fueling the fire within. There was work to be done.

I began by gathering scraps of clothing that were littered all around the room and soaked them in the water before wrapping my body diligently. Granted, some of the guys had wandered their way down to the chamber to see what the fuss was about because firing a firearm does that…and it sucks when you don't have a suppressor. I was no MacGyver, by any means. I was just proficient…in eradicating my tormentors, and hopefully getting the hell out of this place. So a pair of the guys came in, and I did the only thing I could think of to make sure I didn't miss; play possum. It is surprising how many goons fall for that trick. I mean, I always thought it was hilarious in movies; or where you're sitting there watching, and you're like "Don't move! Play dead! Go for the surprise!" kind of deal. I also suppose it's a bit sad for those lunkheads. In a way but to Hell with them. They asked for it by all the monstrosities and atrocities they had committed. I laid sprawled on the floor, the gun under my leg. That's it, take a few more steps you dumb thick fu—. A few shots and they both went down. I'll admit, I laughed and was amazed at myself and also the artistry of the way they both landed; one's head in the other's crotch. I felt the need to say something witty, but I had slightly more pressing matters to tend to.

As I 'walked' to the exit of the room, armed to the teeth with all my captor's weapons of choice, I thought of how I was going to go about fleeing. Do I unlock all the cells and free the people now? Do I kill everyone that dares attack me? Do I flee and get help from the authorities? There were so many scenarios and problematic instances with each one…my head began to ache. I figured, 'let's just play it by ear.'

After some more thought, I figured "let's let the bulls run." I began opening the locks with haste. I could hear footsteps; they were rushing down the stairs from the crucible above. The people screamed...oh, did they scream! Such cries for bloody vengeance. A few of them darted for the torture room to arm themselves, while others fled to the stairs. It was there, where the guys met the tidal wave of retribution. The now-freed-captives butchered their captors; smashing their heads against the stone stairs, the stoned walls, each other. Hell, some of the people even tore their tormentor's throats out; either with their bare hands, or teeth. The sight didn't disturb me as I watched on wielding the flashlight. In fact, I smiled at their disfiguring and dismembering.

I roamed down the corridor, stepping over the bodies of the fallen captors. Some even pleaded for help! Ha! The folks would take care of those left behind, or let them die their just deserved slow and painful death. Soon I'd finally find my way to the arena....and boy oh boy, was it in sheer chaos. It was glorious! Doors and pens for the dogs, pigs, and other animals burst open. Dogs turned on their masters, tearing out their throats, clawing out their eyes, tearing their limbs off. Pigs swarmed the Herder, trampling and devouring him. Rats swarmed their master, Timmy Dementia; gnawing on his face, eyes, nose, ears, and body. Crows flocked and swarmed their former masters; pecking out their eyes, tongues, and lips. The lions, tigers, and bears roared fiercely as they saluted, and slaughtered The Pink Brothers. There were people everywhere. It was an arena jammed full of people spilling each other's blood. It was absolute chaos, anarchy…revenge. It was…beautiful.

As I made my way across the crucible, there came a man's boisterous voice over the PA system. "Spoiled little children! I give you a home, food, water, and a place to sleep—and this is how you repay me? No, no, there will be none of this! No more, I say! Those of you that return to your cells may be forgiven, but if you do not…if you do not obey your lord, and master—" the voice trailed off, to the sound of a series of mechanical whirls that filled the arena. Time seemed to slow down, to me at least.

The arena erupted into a horrendous growl of gunfire. Bullets ripped through people and beasts alike. I 'ran' as fast as I could. Screams, horrifying cries, and blood filled the crucible. I did not know who this…lord and master were. Maybe someone had assumed the mantle over The Boss? Maybe there was already a coup d'état in place, and I just fouled things up? Whatever the case, I was royally fucked, and hiding under a dead black bear. I watched women, children, man, and beast get torn to pieces with the explosive onslaught. After about a minute, the gunfire stopped.

The voice then spoke again over the PA system. "Disobedient children…look at what you've made me do?!" The voice then sighed, "No matter. You are all forgiven. As I am a loving, kind, and gentle lord, and master. However, it will take some time to rebuild—" the voice then seemed to go off on a distant and not-all-there, kind of rant.

The man was old. Really old. I looked around the crucible to see if I could find out where they were; the thought of perhaps dispatching them from afar came to mind. I didn't see any of the guys around. I also hoped that maybe some folk either still lived downstairs, or had already pressed on; escaping this hellish prison. As I wondered and pondered, there came the voice next to me…my opportunity, my wish granted!

"And you, dear child, you are the catalyst in this rebellion?" Spoke the ancient, frail man. He was bald, with pure white tufts of hair that peppered the back of his scalp, and formed his beard. His eyes blue; rich and pure, like a fresh, bright spring day. He was dressed in a golden robe and worn sandals. He held his weight on a solid brown oak staff. I was awestruck that such an old man was so malevolent and cruel.

"I never wanted to be taken. I am only trying to go home—to find my wife and kids." I replied, pushing the bear's dead body off me.

The old man nodded. "None of us are ever asked to be taken, my dear boy. We are all the same as we come in, and the same when we leave. Nothing more, nothing less."

I was puzzled by the old man's way with words. "What do you mean?"

He turned and took a few steps, kneeling beside the barely breathing bear. "You see this beast?" I nodded. "His name was Johan. He has been born several thousand times, and soon will be again." He patted the bear's head, "Rest, my child, rest." The bear then took its final breath. The old man stood once again, straight and true. "I could name these animals and people…even you, Edward."

"I…I don't understand. You are talking madness!"

"Yes, yes, I suppose. However, I ask you this. You have no memories of being taken, do you not?"

"I…it's all a blur. I can't really." I shook my head. It began to ache tremendously.

"What you remember, are the bits and pieces." The old man smiled. "You see, when we are taken, we lose fragments of our mind…our memories. Only when we are free, do we see everything clearly; the whole picture comes into focus, the movie played without the intermissions." He grunted as he sat down before me.

I began to weep. "All the pain…all of the suffering. What did you have them do to us?!"

Still did the old man smile. "I had them do nothing that life hadn't prepared for you already. These people died needlessly…however, they didn't die needlessly."

"Why do you speak in riddles?! You are making no sense," I yelled at him as I collapsed to my knees.

"You claim Hell would offer much respite, and yet, you claimed to suffer tremendously here; feeling the suffering of others—their hate, anger, sadness, despair—such emotions and actions that you shared with both victim, and murderer. You've created this world. You alone. You. Are. Alone."

As the words seemed to ring like a thunderous gong, the people and beasts disappeared. Everything faded until it was just the old man and me under the warm, vibrant sunlight, on a tall grassy hill. "I understand now."

The old man smiled brightly. "You needn't hang on anymore, Edward. You are free to go home whenever you want. You needn't build a prison to confine yourself to. You can stay and fight, and perhaps…perhaps awaken. Awaken to another fight. Or you can make peace with yourself. Let the guilt, the pain, and end your suffering that you've endured for all these years."

I remembered it all…I was in a car accident some time ago with my wife and kids—the kids were killed by a drunk driver, while I remained in a coma…for how long, I don't know. My wife would come to visit time to time…but she took her life at my bedside. My eyes were always open to the truth, but it hurt so bad that I eventually had closed them after that because the world outside could no longer offer me comfort.

"Home…" I had long since forgotten the meaning. I cried a little bit. "You know me all too well, stranger, but I haven't the foggiest of who you are."

The old man smiled brilliantly, "Death knows no strangers, my boy."

I looked up to the sun, its warmth so inviting. I knew it was a lie, but I knew where I was going. "I'd like to go home then."

The old man nodded and sat there. "Soon you shall."

I closed my eyes, as a gentle breeze wafted over my body. A perplexed kaleidoscope of memories of mine own and those of my past existences came to one; the beginning, and now the end…at least this time around. As it ended—the encroaching darkness that would be only for a minute—there I saw the three faces I could only ever know. For I would soon be home.

In the outside world, the machines that helped sustain life beeped maniacally; sounding the alarm at the races—known as life. Doctors, nurses, and other hospital personnel rushed to save the male adult named Edward Croix. He died on a Monday, at 3:18 pm. He was 46.

The Wheel of Torment

THE THERAPIST LOOKED THROUGH the notepad and file on his newest patient. He hadn't looked her over, yet as he was still thumbing through the contents of the rather large file. Her name was Jessica Flynn, or as she was known to the public as "The Girl That Was Saved by God."

The therapist's bushy dark brown eyebrows raised and fell. Sweat built upon his brow as he flipped through more pages. The small black wire-rimmed glasses occasionally fogged up. He couldn't believe it himself.

Poor thing, he thought.

As he readjusted in his dark green leather chair, crossing the right leg over the left, and fixed his black slacks to hide the dull gray socks that burrowed into the brown loafers.

He let out a hacking cough. "Ahem, ah, excuse me, Miss Flynn."

She did not reply.

A bead of sweat fell onto his glasses from his brow and trickled down to his cheek. He removed them and wiped them against his black and gray sweater. He cleared his throat, as he set to replace the glasses. His brown eyes attempted at focusing on the blurred image of Ms. Flynn, then back down to the papers in front of him.

"Now, Ms. Flynn, can you start by telling me what troubles you, and why you are here?"

A soft voice replied, "I am troubled because I am alive, and I am here because I survived."

The therapist stroked his chin. "I see. And how is it that you see yourself as being troubled by your liveliness?"

"When you have seen what I have seen and been what I have been through, there's just some things that you cannot let go of—no, some things that cannot let go of you."

The therapist nodded. "Please, in your own words, tell me of what troubles you...and what you experienced."

After a long pause. Jessica looked down at the floor with the same blue eyes that observed so many years ago.

"Ten years ago, I survived one of the most brutal, horrific, and terrifying events in my life. I still have haunting nightmares of it—disturbing visions, things you could not possibly comprehend."

She stared blankly up at the wild brown-haired therapist that sat before her.

"Go on," said the man.

"In the backyard of the hundred-acre wood farm. A red brick ranch with a cellar where...they kept us in. There were other people too, kids, parents...I forget how many exactly. We were all locked up. There lived a family...a family of religious zealots...fanatics—they had brainwashed their oldest daughter. Their only son tried to rebel and make them see to reason...but he was struck down for disobeying his father."

Her eyes fell to the floor again. She recanted the sight of blood—so, so much blood. "They called it...'The Wheel of Torment.'"

Jessica paused after the words. She remembered it all. Before her did the structure start to assemble itself, and before her, did the room begin to change into that day so many years ago.

The man began to sweat more profusely and said nothing.

She took a deep breath and began to tell of the event.

****

"We have to figure a way out!" A man whispered to another in the dark.

"Shh! Quiet! You'll get us killed, and then there won't be a way out!" he replied harshly.

"We're going to die anyway! Wouldn't you rather die fighting than just rolling over and dying to these—these lunatics?!"

The man tried persuading the other, and other people to come together and overpower their captors.

Up above, heavy footsteps could be heard that came close to the door that led down to them.

"Be thankful they haven't chained us up yet." A man whispered.

The footsteps stopped at the door. The door opened wide to let in the bright light that they all yearned for.

A tall man's silhouette asked aloud down to the dark. "Y'all not tryin' to plan an escape now, are ya?"

"N—no, sir. We're being good, real good." A few people replied.

"That's good, real good of you, children." The old man grinned up on the stairs. "I have some good news for y'all. Y'all gonna be goin' home today."

A commotion erupted from within the cellar, praises, thanks, and other useless banter.

The man stomped the floor with the butt end of his hunting rifle. "Now, now! Shut yer traps! Don't need all this whoopin' and hollerin'."

"Please, Jebediah, let us go home, please." A woman pleaded.

"Momma, I'm hungry." A child whispered.

"Now, don't cha worry a thing. For you see, I've heard from the good Lord above, and he said it's time...time to send his flock on home. I be seein' to that soon." Jebediah slowly closed the door and locked it.

While some praised and believed they were going to be free, others questioned the motives of the man.

"What the hell does he mean by that?" A man whispered.

"They're going to kill us—they're going to kill us all!" A man began to sob hysterically.

"Shh, shut up! You're going to get us killed with that nonsense right there!"

Outside, in the backyard near the big red pole barn there stood the prize of the Everby's. It began to whirl and come to life.

Jebediah smiled at his creation of salvation. He wiped the sweat from his brow with his dirty white handkerchief. He looked up at the sun through his reddened fingers. He took out his pocket watch and looked at the time. The hands neared noon. He caught a glimpse of his blue eyes, worn, and sunburnt face. Sparse white flecks popped up through the black tufts of hair. He looked down at the ground, then closed the watch.

The time had finally come.

He looked over at his wife. "You know, you are the light of my day, and the world to me, don't cha?"

"I sure do." The older woman smiled softly and gave Jeb a kiss and hugging him tightly.

She was short, pale, with brown eyes like the earth. Graying blonde hair that was let down ran past her waist. With a gray and white dress, and black buckled shoes with white stockings.

"Dahlia, be a dear and get Annie out here, will ya?"

"Sure thing, sweetheart," she replied giving him a pat on his belly.

Moments later, Annie, their daughter came out from the house. "You called, Pa?"

Jebediah looked his daughter over and smiled brightly, and full. "You sure are the sweetest thing, darlin'."

Annie had just turned eighteen some days back. She had bright blonde hair that was tightly done in a bun. Her bright green eyes shine brilliantly in the sunny day, comparable to her pale complexion. She wore a light blue dress with white frills, and black belt buckled shoes, with white stockings.

"Aw, thank you, pa," she blushed. "Did y'all need me for something?"

"Well, Annie my dear. The day is today that we meet our maker. The day we go home. I want you to get everyone ready and up here. Your Ma will help ya, in case any of them get ideas. Now, don't be keepin' the good Lord awaitin'."

"Yes, Pa, right away," she nodded and ventured inside with her mother.

****

"So, it's agreed then. We jump them and make a stand. Right?" A man whispered to others.

"What about the children?" A woman asked.

"If we can get rid of them, the kids will be fine." The alleged leader replied.

"I don't think they'd actually hurt the kids. Would they," another woman questioned.

"For crying out loud, they killed their own son! What makes you think they won't do the same to your boy?" he turned his head to the dark silhouettes that stood around him, "or your girls? Your family. They're going to kill us all unless we do something."

"Mommy, I'm scared," a little girl sobbed, clinging to her mother.

"There, there, don't worry. You'll be OK, J-bug. Ya hear? You have to be strong." Her mother replied.

They heard the mechanical whirring that was so profound. It immediately struck fear into the heart of the captives.

"What the hell is that?!"

Then, the doors that led outside began to unlock and shuffle. Daylight pierced the darkness of the cellar. Before them stood Annie and Dahlia.

The people all crowded together and clung to one another. Children cried among themselves, while the few families that were still together huddled close together.

Eyes darted all over the place—the Everby's and the captives. In a corner, a young boy began to whisper a prayer to himself while rocking.

"Alright, folks, y'all free to go... Come out one at a time, though, ya hear?" Dahlia said.

No one dared move.

"What's the matter? Y'all don't want to go home? See your friends and family? Kids?" Dahlia looked about.

"Listen up and listen good, if y'all don't come on out of there, I'll just shoot ya dead where ya be. Now, get out here in the light, or else!" She hollered.

Slowly, some people began to stir and make their way up the steps to the outside world.

As a woman slowly climbed to the top of the steps with her son, she looked at Annie and at Dahlia. "Please, please let us go," she sobbed.

"Sweetheart, I plan to, don't cha worry your pretty little head," Dahlia replied. "Now, I suggest you get to steppin' if ya know what's good for ya." She waved a handgun at the mother and son.

Annie hosed the pair down with water and mumbled something incoherently aloud. The couple—startled—kept on their path that laid before them. Before them was a dirt path that led to a monstrous construct.

Here it stood... "The Wheel of Torment." Namely, so for its slaughtering capabilities. A wooden construct, woven with wrought iron that was about ten feet or so tall. Several wheels that spun in different directions from one another, with approximately a six-foot radius, with several rows of iron and wooden tips. They were already bloodied and severely dull (probably by the prior use on their cattle sometime prior). In the center was a loud motor that whirled and roared with extensive and precise components. Below it was a drainage pit that was dug out that only the artisan knew where to. Years of tempering and pride decorated this killing machine, and it awaited new blood to feast on.

Nearby, Jebediah stood with his hands clasped together, mumbling aloud something incoherent.

The mother and son cried to one another and pleaded with Annie and Dahlia. Their pleas, however, only fell upon deaf ears.

"Get steppin'. Be a good momma and lead. Make an example for your boy," Dahlia yelled.

More of the other captives rose up from the cellar and saw what a sick and twisted idea the Everby's considered "going home," and "being sent free."

A group of men looked at one another. Dahlia had turned her back on them all, while Annie continued to hose down the next lot.

"It's now or never," one man whispered to the other.

In a surge of adrenaline, the men rushed Dahlia and Annie. One motioned to take the woman hostage, but their uprising was quickly dispersed.

"Momma, behind you," Annie yelled.

Dahlia cried out for Jeb while fending off her attackers. She fired off a few rounds that struck one man in the leg, and several shots in another's chest.

During the commotion, the mother sent her son to flee to the woods.

Jeb quickly pulled out his revolver and shot the attacking men dead, square in the head, and lost sight of the boy.

"Now, look at what you made me do! Look at what you made me do!" Jeb walked over and clubbed the mother in the back of the head.

A few of the men that still were alive groaned in pain. "Take them," Jebediah ordered.

"Any of you idjits move, you'll be shot dead. Got it?"

The others nodded and sobbed at the failed attempt.

"We could still try," a woman whispered to some of the others.

A woman shook her head, "I've already made my peace. I rather not have anyone's blood on my hands, let alone mine on theirs. These bastards will rot in Hell."

Jeb cursed to himself at the boy's escape. Still, they were miles and miles from any water and any civilization. He figured the boy wouldn't survive long.

"Annie, are you OK, darlin'? Jeb asked.

"Yes, Pa, I'm fine," she replied.

"Good girl. Go get the camera," Jeb ordered.

Annie came back moments later with a video camera and brought it to her father.

"Thank you, sweetie. You've been the best daughter any father could ever hope to have." Jeb kissed his daughter's forehead and gave her a tight hug.

Jeb called to his wife. "Dahlia, be a dear and get one of them youngins to c'mere and film, will ya?"

She took the camera and found a girl that was clinging to her mother's raggedy clothes. She ushered the child over to a chair that was under a branch. On its end, there hung a noose. Dahlia fashioned the rope around the young girl's neck and bound her feet to the chair. "Now, listen here, darlin'. You're gonna stand over here and keep the camera goin'. You sit down or try anything, your neck's gonna snap like a twig, ya hear me?"

The girl nodded and sobbed.

"Now, stop that, Pa's gonna say your prayers, ya hear? You're gonna go to a good place." Dahlia 'assured' the girl.

The girl looked over at her mother, who cried and only looked on.

Jeb drug the mother of the escaped boy's body to the wheel of torment. A horrible sound of bones snapping and popping ensued. Everyone cried in unison, save for the Everby's.

"Praise the Lord, for He is great," Jeb yelled.

"We have to do something," a woman whispered to the remaining adults.

"Now, do it now," a woman bellowed.

"Jeb! Jeb!" The women tackled Dahlia to the ground and began savagely beating her, and wrestled the gun free.

Jeb aimed and fired at the woman that beat his wife into the ground, but she continued to wail on the hag. He continued to shoot, emptying the remaining rounds in the woman. Finally, the bullet-riddled woman collapsed atop Dahlia, while the other got the gun and fired wildly at the fast approaching Jebediah. Several shots missed, but finally one struck him in the midsection, but nothing fatal. Jeb unsheathed his hunting knife and ran it deep through the woman's gut.

Some of the children wagered to run themselves, but that effort was stifled as Annie had grabbed Jeb's hunting rifle and began picking off some of the runners and gathered ammunition for Jeb.

"Y'all don't even know what you're doin'!? You keep makin' efforts at livin' and for what? To maybe live a few more days? Ain't nobody comin' to save ya. Ain't nobody, but the good Lord above! Accept Him, and repent," Jeb yelled.

Bodies were dragged back to the wheel. More and more were added to the bloody 'succotash.' The young girl had stopped crying now. She had accepted her fate. She debated, though, die from hanging, or to die to the wheel? She prayed to herself, as she looked through the lens and focused on the body of her mother that was now being tossed onto the wheel. A spike penetrated her skull and gut, while her limbs were broken several ways and she was left flopping about. Others began their walk towards the grinder...and were shoved to their fate.

"Dear Lord, I pray to you. I, Jebediah Raymond Everby, giveth unto you, my only daughter, Annie Carrol Everby. For she is your faithful and loyal servant." Jeb led Annie to the wheel. "I love you, darlin'."

"I love you too, Pa...Ma," Annie replied, giving each of her parents a hug and kiss.

She took a few steps, and then stopped just before the wheel. After a moment, she leaped upon it. A spike penetrated through her skull, ripping her scalp apart, grinding her limbs to loose 'appendages.' More meat for the grinder.

"Now, let ye sinners repent," Jeb hollered aloud.

One by one, he, and Dahlia begin to toss children to the mechanical beast. Their small bodies were engulfed wholly. Tiny arms, legs, and bodies were impaled, ripped, and torn apart. Some are lucky to die, while others continue to spin on the spokes and suffer an agonizing death. Round and round they go, watching others come to blow.

The girl filming focused on another little girl: her arm snapped in several places, legs twisted and dangling, with an iron stud through her right cheek. The blood of others poured over her pale face and long dark blonde hair. She cried in pain, wanting to be shot, but Jeb and Dahlia did nothing. Shortly after that, the girl died.

The constant sound of bone snapping and blood bursting. The clay earth became redder—a deep pool of crimson where the dead that aren't still riding the wheel now laid. Intestines continuously wound up, being unwound from the stomachs of innocents—a wicked weaving of death...and murder.

"Praise the Lord! Praise Him for He is just!" Dahlia bellowed.

Blood sprayed against Jeb and Dahlia's faces.

"My dear, it's time." Jeb sighed, catering to his wound.

The little girl continued to film, watching as Jeb and Dahlia tied a rope to one another. He embraced Dahlia and hurled one end of the line at the Wheel of Torment. Together, they were dragged along the ground, until they met the monstrosity they created.

Several moments passed, the girl continued to hold the camera. She started to sob and thought she was alone. A dark blonde hair girl atop one of the spikes of the wheel mumbled to her incoherently. She turns the camera around and gives a statement.

Small blue eyes filled with dried tears and reddened from crying. Her brown hair flows with the wind that gently runs through it. Her thin, pale face bruised.

"My name is Laurie Endrid. I am nine years old. My parents were Nancy and Thomas Endrid. My brother was Thomas Patrick Endrid, Jr. He's the one on the bottom...next to Jenny. I can stand no longer. May God have mercy on my soul and forgive me for the choice I am about to make. Lord, I pray to you that Jebidiah and Dahlia Everby will pay for their crimes against all of us—for their 'sacrifice' to you."

She continued to stare into the camera for a moment, taking deep breaths, hesitant. Finally, the camera dropped to the ground.

****

In the memory playback in her mind, much like the video, Jessica watched Laurie struggle, gasping for air—her feet kicking wildly. At last, they came to rest, and her body swayed with the wind of the chilly spring day. She remembers the wheel breaking and falling into the bloody pit, among all the bodies, and hearing the sounds of helicopters, and cars swarming the farm not too long after.

"The F.B.I. and other governmental agencies had been tracking the Everby's. They were too late, though. Mostly everyone was dead—save for Laurie, but she can't do much nowadays, nor does she like to talk...about things." She paused, "and the boy who got away. They found him on the way there."

She looked down at the ground, her left eye and cheek ached. "Sometimes, people make fun of me for my scars—" her voice trailed off. "Though I don't have my real leg and arm anymore, I can still feel the pain. Often times, I wonder why I survived and not some of the others. I guess, perhaps, I just had to see it through."

Sweat had built upon the man's brow, while his heart raced, "I am so sorry, Jessica," the therapist apologetically said.

He looked up at her from the file, wiping the sweat from his brow with his palm. He remembered the girl that shared the same dark cellar with him.

Jessica replied with a broken smile, "I'm just glad that you made it out, Brian."

Cure for Pain

I T WOULD BE HERE, in this room where they'd find him. There would be no letter, no prim and proper folded attempt at saying goodbye; nothing to leave behind, nothing to say or to pass on. It was to be his goodbye. The radio held its farewell ceremony, commencing its invisible fanfare as it sounded off from the corner of the bare apartment living room. The young man strolled to the center of the living room to claim his 'award.' He grinned at the thought of such a blasphemous act that would soon come to pass in such a place. All of the blinds were clenched shut—save for the sparse traces of light that fought eagerly to pierce through the darkened veil of the once lively red room. He had turned over the photos of many friends, and family. He didn't want to have their eyes change his mind, to further judge and condemn him. He had laughed the loudest out of all his friends, and would go out of his way to bring a smile to people all around. As of late, though, he was now tired of the facade.

A crumpled cigarette laid smoldering in a crystal-clear ashtray—that last final puff before no more. He took one last shot of whiskey; the almighty liquid courage and then threw the glass against the wall—shattering it into pieces, and with that…he continued on to complete his destiny. He stared at the pair of freshly polished black leather combat boots that sat patiently on the cherry oak chair in the center of the room. "Death's boots," as his granddad described them. "One day, they'll be yours…and one day they'll be what you wear to your grave." He smiled at the shared memory.

The young man recanted the immortalized memory on the eve of his passing thirteen days ago. "My boy, we're all part of a grand orchestra; one where we each have a piece to play, and one that we play to an unknown conductor. Some sections are rivals; some don't like what the other plays, but all in all, it's a massive classical masterpiece we all play. When the music gets too loud, we have the ability to turn it down. Some do; some don't. Some quit the band, while others try to stick it out. Me? Why I've been playing the same tune now for 92 years. When the chorus ends…well…that's when I'd like to go."

More and more memories began to seep from the long-sealed vault. His world was upside down. His family was left in shambles. All his friends were scattered like ashes to the four winds. While his love was some thousand miles away.

The young man put the boots on, one at a time, and laced them to perfection before tucking his blue jeans in. He wiped the few specs of ashes that had clung to his white t-shirt for life, smearing them into a gray oblivion.

His mother often reminded him to "get rid of those damned boots!" That, "they took your Pop and Poppy, and with the way you're shaping up to be, they'll take you too!" He stood atop the chair, tall, confident, and readied the rope that hung in front of him, placing his head through the noose he had diligently made. It wasn't her fault. It wasn't anyone's. It was his choice, and remedy to cure the pain.

Then, an old song came on as he had made his last gesture. It seemed to increase in volume until it flooded the darkened room. It seemed to speak to him, retelling the tale of his life: its highs and lows, of the dark and light. Where one group sang of what he could do, while another told him what to do. Music had helped so much in his darkest of times, but as of late, it did not have as much effect as it once had. He found no joy in the things he had come to know, in people, in places, or things.

His eyes sweltered with tears; the confusion set in, along with panic, and fear. He could feel a presence behind the front door, one that would barge in, and assure him everything will be alright—to come home and stop the pain. He could hear a voice on the end of the line tell him it's OK, that there are things worth fighting for, living for people, places, that life has a meaning. He could feel eyes outside the window, ones that struggled to penetrate the barrier to make their plea; to make him turn around, come down and talk about it. That maybe tomorrow would be better, just have a little patience, and it'll be alright. That this apartment, and this life—his life—was not only a prison.

However, there was no one. No one was behind the door. No voice on the other end of the unplugged line. No eyes that attempted to sway his choice. He was alone. He would soon be a memory…a voice…an image to be stored away in the dusty minds of multimedia, people, and books. He would be gone and forgotten—save for being a statistic. For what he would come to face; whether it be a religious deity, a void of nothingness, or an afterlife, he'd face it alone.

The chair gave way, and here he swam in the middle of the room. He struggled to pull himself above the sea of blackness, but it only continued to push him down. A kaleidoscope of colors and shapes played out before him, with memories of old flashing vividly one last time on his minds faulty camera, which then led him to darkness. The music slowly played on, while the dying choir sang of his final moments in the ever-growing dismal and abysmal background.

Sunlight pierced the darkness, stirring him to his senses. He could note the mumbling voices and sobbing that echoed all around. He found himself in a hospital bed with people now huddling over him, most of them with tears that streamed down their cheeks, their eyes red and heavy. Everyone had come. He wasn't alone. No one quarreled with one another. No one laid blame. No one criticized, judged, or condemned him. They all pleaded for him to stay, to live renewed, and gave praise to his love that had come to surprise him at his apartment.

Meanwhile, in the corner of the room, there stood a silhouette of a tall, slender man in a long black coat by the window. He had a square ghostly face, with wild feathered short black hair, and gray eyes. He gazed out to the world beyond. He took note and turned to the young man's attention as he puffed on a cigarette. Slowly did the figure exit the bustling room; however, on his way out, he turned down the volume on the radio that echoed the same tune before, giving a slight nod before leaving. Whether it was in his mind or not, the words resounded, and the young man couldn't help but smile in thanks to the mysterious stranger.

Next to his bedside, on the floor, there sat Death's boots; its laces crisscrossed, forming a makeshift smile—welcome back.

Dead Echo

IN A SMALL BEDROOM, there sat a young man on the edge of the bed—rocking. He held his head heavy in his hands. His eyes were clenched shut, and streams of salty tears rolled down his flushed cheeks. Small tufts of sandy brown hair poked through his pale fingers as he slid them front to back. In his troubled mind, invisible knots twisted together, binding themselves tightly.

The doorknob began to twist and rattle violently. The muffled voices behind it demanded his attention; their suspicion having been aroused and they had laid blame on him for the crime.

"Leave me alone! What more do you want from me?!" the young man pleaded.

Silence did not fall. The turmoil only strengthened the problematic matter and increased the tension within. While the persistent pounding on the door and shouting from the other side seemed to subside, subtle thoughts had begun to seep from his mind. They surged and destroyed the dam he had so foolishly tried to build. It had not even been a week since.

A smile scrawled across his lips as two familiar figures pierced the veil before him—a woman and child—both came to his side. Distinguished with old garments, yet held a holy presence. A bright light radiated around them, bathing him in a golden glow that soothed his troubled mind. However, it did not disclose their faces, yet he knew who they were.

The woman's voice echoed in his mind—offering comfort, and it so soothed and loosened the bindings within. "Eventually, you will have to confront them. It wasn't your fault. Hiding and locking yourself up will not solve the pain or allow you to be rid of it."

The man lifted up his now light head, gazing upon the familiars. The thoughts continued to swell and overwhelm him. Memories vividly flashed on the back of his eyeballs—like a replay of a home movie. When days and times were better when he had it all. He rubbed his eyes as they began to swell up with tears—the tears of remembrance. Before his mind's eye was a young woman—his wife— holding their little girl in her arms. Fashioned in typical casual attire, he grinned, how relaxed she always was. Her long black hair covered her face, cuddling close to the giggling girl who sat on her lap. Their daughter— in her small white spring gown—glowing much like her long golden locks just like they did when they'd shine brilliantly on that bright sunny summer day at the park. They both smiled back at the man.

His daughter's voice echoed, "I love you, daddy!"

While his wife giggled with her bright smile, "I love you, baby."

Screams soon followed after that. Horrible, excruciatingly painful screams followed by gunshots. As the memory finished playing back, he began to sob uncontrollably, repeating, "I'm so sorry! Please forgive me!" Soon, the vision dispersed before him, as he sat rocking back and forth. "I'd do anything— anything to have you back. Anything to be with you both again. I'd give up anything and everything."

Simultaneously, the doorknob and door continued to shake and rattle violently.

Again, the woman spoke. "There is one way…"

He closed his eyes as the voice spoke with assurance, and nodded to himself. He picked himself up and shuffled over to the dresser that stood in solitude before where he once sat. He opened the top drawer and pushed the many socks aside. Finally, his quest came to a complete as he removed the small handgun from the dresser and held it firmly in his hand. He looked it over making sure it was suitable for the job he had intended. Once assured it was fit and ready for its final stand, the young man calmly walked over to the window.

He gazed out into the outside world, where the trees were vibrant with the verdant fertility of life swaying in its breath. The harmonization of the birds singing to everyone, everywhere. The sun's last caress bathed his face. Finally, the door buckled weakened from the continuous pounding of many fists and obscured words. He looked the gun over once more and then shifted his sight back outside.

The door exploded open as the navy-blue blob rushed in. The young man turned about and aimed lazily at the million-eyed blob that drew as many arms in return for him. The man fired a shot with the gun; purposefully missing. The blob returned fire— one hundred-fold—upon him, resulting in the man falling to the floor.

As the warmth of life and its breath began to leave him, the familiar figures came once more— mother and child. Tears that laid in the waiting rolled off onto the floor, coagulating with the blood that pooled beneath him; comparable to the cherry hardwood floor. The blob surrounded his dying body. Some took note of toy gun that laid in the man's hand, while bits and pieces broke off and ran out of the room to retrieve a pair of white cells to attempt to treat his wounds, but it was all for naught.

The young man laid with a smile as all the pain evaporated. His head became light, his vision now blurred, and all feeling had left his body. His last sight was that of finally returning to the arms of his familiar loves—his loving wife and daughter.

The End's Messenger

TO SAY. "IT WAS A DARK and stormy night," like how so many stories had begun, would be considered an understatement. This night was indeed a testament of nature's wrath…and beauty. The inked sky was full of irregular crackling javelins of light that blazed across the darkened heavens. In its wake was an absolute drenching rain that could soak down to the marrow of man. The winds—rabid and vicious—roared and clawed at all that would dare stand in its path. Thunder bellowed its horn of war, resonating as it rolled throughout the mortal world. Yes, my friend, this, this was truthfully the storm of the century.

In my ignorance, I shrugged it off as a typical phenomenon. I walked away from the large picture window, to retire to the rosewood leather chair by the fireplace (having been satisfied with my gaze out into the bewildering twilight). I lit the cigar I had retrieved earlier, happenstance upon the weather's dastardly interruption. I crossed my legs; the silk pajamas lightly ruffled in the elegance and comfort. Here, I sat alone in the dark study. The flicker of the flames bathed the room in a soft orange intravenously with a yellow contrast. The crimson walls were now more vibrant in their hue, as the flames' light made the shadows dance upon the walls. Warmth radiated from the resurging power of the fire in the study. I observed the flames that danced the most tribal of nature while others feasted upon the wood's carcass. The room flooded with the constant contest of fire and wind, it all overwhelmed my ears.

As I fixated further upon the flames, I could hear the howls of the wind and the roar of the fire become as fluent as any spoken word. Where then the fire soon took on a form: a face, a slender, and curvaceous body slowly. Here…before me now was there ever such beauty and grace! I remained seated, paralyzed…speechless. Whether it was fear or curiosity that struck my fancy, the enchantress with an elegant face flickered, as it withheld its splendor.

A soft, enticing whisper echoed in my mind beckoning me nearer. "Servant of life and flesh, heed the call. War is upon the world! The end of days is to come to pass!"

The pure marble yellow-orange-white glossed with intent—such fixated—she stared deep into my eyes, like a lioness's gaze upon her prey. My eyes swelled with disbelief; I was dumbstruck.

I turned my gaze away, having become lost in thoughts that raced, where I was led into the depths of my mind—I scrambled and sought the doors for answers, all of which were empty. I turned to face the fatal attraction. I knelt close to the siren, and she revealed visions that flooded my mind of what would soon come to pass. The whisper, now disembodied, echoed once more.

"Man's life is to come to an end. True retribution is at hand. The time...is nigh. It is the time that all mortals fear of—the end. However, all is not lost, for the world will be reborn. Fire shall cleanse the impurities. The scarring that evil has left upon the face of the earth shall be purified. The pure shall be soothed and reconciled, from which they shed from. The judgment on high has been passed. The cogs of the new future have begun to turn. To advise the ushering of the forthcoming age: selection, devotion, and truth must endure. For on the first day—fire—purges the impure. Upon the second day, lightning will clash, temper, and reshape. On the third, the wind— strengthens and seals. On the final day, water shall cleanse and further purify. A new day will then emerge, marking the era of a true beginning. It is on this day. The chosen are relinquished of slumber and returned. Where then upon the next, those that committed such aggravated acts against the name of life will sprout and also begin anew."

These events were told, bold and genuine. The wind rang soft and pure in my ears. As I stood erect before the unknown enchanting messenger, enthralled, blinded, I nodded in acknowledgment of my task.

Slowly the life-giving inferno soothes its rage and dies. The once sultry temptress now turned to ash before me. The soft glowing embers wriggle, writhe, and squirm, before erupting wildly into a hint of a new spark of life.

A smile crossed my face while a tear fell. I retired to my chair to finish my cigar while the blaze around me consumes the world, and I. I am soon greeted and embraced by a long-lost love. My eyes close as I am relinquished of all wrong.

Lightning continues to play its concerto while fire and the wind elegantly waltz while the rain riddled the dark ash with its pure tears—the embers lying dormant.

The end had come...just as it was foretold by the tempest temptress messenger.

For Mom

A COOL CRISP SUMMER BREEZE swept across her face, only to escape and disperse over the mirror-like lake. Azure seemed to stretch on eternally all around from where she sat. Rolling verdant hills sprawled everywhere, nestled in the small cove she had come to know only recently, with flowers of exotic properties and those of familiarity sprung from the earthly womb. Birds chirped and sang of a perfect day.

She sheltered herself under the care of a lone red oak tree; similar as the one that had once stood in her backyard but had been cut down, a stump remained. She pressed herself against the trunk of the massive tree, absorbing the beauty of nature that surrounded herself. Her head dropped slightly, to her hands where she clung to a silver locket. Inside was a black and white picture of another woman. Although it was drained of color, she knew the features well: middle-aged, with the same long golden hair that was passed onto her. Azure eyes that sparkled radiantly in the days blessed sun. She closed her eyes in remembrance.

Mom...

A lone tear escaped from the young woman's eye and rolled down her cheek; then falling onto her pale sundress. She opened her eyes, slowly coming to her feet; wandering to the lake that sprawled before her.

A tiny wood dock made its way out into the water. Wrangled to one of the posts, there was a small crimson cedar boat that waltzed to the subtle ways of the soothing waters. The young woman climbed aboard the vessel, unhitching her watery steed, slowly riding out into the middle of the lake. She recalled what her mother had used to sing to her when she was little: *Someone's rocking my dreamboat, someone's invading my dream. We were sailing along, so peaceful and calm, suddenly something went wrong.*

It was here she found peace; the sadness subsided. This was what they had done in the past together; to rid their worries and shake the world's problems loose from their minds. She closed her eyes, swaying in the Earth's breath. Swirling in the pool of life...and death; a precious flower that trembled.

Someone's rocking my dreamboat, disturbing the beautiful dream. It's a mystery to me, this mutiny at sea, who can it be?

The sky blurred; swirls of gray and white intermingled. The soft breath became a panicked huff. The blue was stripped at its roots, leaving only black and gray. The heavens bellowed with anger and fury. Arcs of pure white lightning snapped, crackled across the skyline. The verdant hills became stripped of life: brown darkened crumpled lumps of the once vibrant.

A friendly breeze gave us a start, to a paradise of our own. All at once a storm blew us apart and left me drifting alone...

A monstrous crash resounded, striking the once mighty red oak tree, sending it into a raging inferno. The wildlife shrieked in agony: birds fell from the sky molting, revolting; from life to death, skeletal remains that landed on the ground. The once beautiful flowers, tore at one each other's throats, spilling a thick black blood upon the leathery brown earth that had begun to flake and resemble skin.

Someone's rocking my dreamboat...

The hills had now become jagged razor teeth, oozing with the putrid pitched blood. The sun finally gave into the darkness; a night of terror had set in.

No stars lighted the way. The light was almost nonexistent, save for the red oak that burned defiantly in the misshapen twilight.

Someone's invading my dream...

The words became louder, consistent with the thunderous roar of thunder, and crash of lightning. The young woman finally opened her eyes to the terror that had befallen the beautiful serenity. Fear, sadness, panic, everything finally set in. Tears of crimson blood rained from the heavens, flooding the blackened waters that furiously thrashed her boat around. She clung to the sides of the vessel, sobbing as to 'why?'

Someone's rocking my dreamboat...

The words echoed now a loud to the dismal world. Darkness encroached more, closer with every passing moment. The red oak had now become ash, blowing to the frenzied winds. Under the pitch water, something lingered. A growl escaped the bubbles that popped at the surface.

Disturbing...our...beautiful...dream...

Laughter escaped, intermingling with the song's words. A maelstrom appeared below the young woman's boat. It pulled her in, along with the darkness. Screams of terror, pleas, and prayers escape from her lips. The frigid waters caught her as the lifeboat was torn to pieces. Absolute cold and darkness engulfed her wholly. The flurry of words, voices, laughter, and growls flooded the waters and her ears—pushing her to the precipice of complete and utter pain.

We were sailing along, so peaceful and calm, suddenly something went wrong.

(it's a mystery to me, this mutiny at the sea, who can it be?)
Drifting alone...
Mystery...
(sea...)
paradise...
(dream...)
Who can it be?
A friendly breeze gave us a start...
Someone's...
(Someone's...)
I'm a captain without any crew...
(Apart...)

alone...

(disturbing...)

you...

She could hear a heartbeat, like when she would place her head upon her mother's chest. Steadily it beat...and slowly...it failed.

Someone's rocking my dreamboat...

(Someone's rocking my dreamboat...)

Someone's invading my dream...

(Someone's disturbing our beautiful dream...)

She could feel familiar arms around her, holding her close. Slowly as the heartbeat became silenced, and did her eyes close, it was at the very end to which she then knew—it was her own.

But with love as my guide, I'll follow the tide, I'll keeping sailing 'til I find...

(you...)

As life had faded, she returned to the waking world. Streams of tears that had rolled down her cheeks had dried up. Her mother's locket still clasped tightly in her hands. She gazed upon at the family group photo that propped itself happily upon her cherry work desk. Attached to it was a somber yellow sticky note that read: Funeral *for Mom. Monday the 18th at 3:18 PM*

Incubus

THE SOMBER GRAY BED SHEETS were torn and tattered. The alabaster covers—ripped by the ravenous razor blade teeth of a demon so putrid. The bondage of body and traitorous mind held repulsed to a shell of its former self. The heartbeat of a horse's gallop, the panicked breathing like that of a mother in labor. The sudden rush and reminisce of life! Ah, Incubus, how were the nights when you would so boldly visit. You first came to me, a child of life and flesh. You tainted my being—possessing my mind with the sweet promise of limitless power and eternity. In return, you granted eternal suffering and torment.

The daily nightmare. Ah, yes. How many people rest their heads on their pillows, tend to, as they say, get their beauty sleep. You come to me, Incubus. The nights of old and new, since I was of the age four or five. You took pleasure in granting me such vividly grotesque and horrifying night terrors—spawning to the world, possessing new beings, and things.

Many people would say, "Oh, well they're just that. Nightmares." Foolish people. Stupid people. Inconceivable and dumbfounded fools! Ah, how I would have loved to have agreed with them. These, however, were more than just that, though. Oh, how you crept into our world, tainting us! The foretold events of the past, present, and future. Mere glimpses of what I've seen from my foresight.

Let it be known that this marks as a testament…of what pain I've endured in the dismemberment of my mind. A fight with myself. A struggle between the forces of good and evil. War stories—of a war on oneself. The tales of love, hate, revenge, death, and life. The age-old question of when we die—if we are judged, and the verdict handed down is eternal damnation and suffering—what is more painful? To experience life all over again, knowing what will happen, and to not able to do a damn thing about it. To live through every day, when you can't change the past, present, or future. To not even be able to destroy yourself…to purge yourself of the pain that is…living. Immortality. Eternal life. What is the point of going on, when everyone around you is taken in time?

And so, he came unto me.

So early, did you first approach me, Incubus. You possessed my toy chest mother had bought for me, didn't you? You crept into the house, deep in the bewitching hour and laid hidden in it the night before. When mother and father had tucked me in, you waited. Dormant did you lay in the small bedroom, smiling at me with your velvet stitching and patches of birds and house. A little light oak bed, 'twas my everlasting resting place. The soft blue plush carpet that weighed upon the back of a quiet beast. The monsters that hid in the small wardrobe were of no concern, for you had already decimated them for me. The chest, yes, it was the chest in which you manifested unto me. It was here, here in which you finally came alive.

Your reign of terror began. There was nothing strange or odd in the day of light. However, in the nightlife, your insatiable hunger manifested and consumed me. Oh, how the many nights were it that you bestowed upon me immortality and eternal damnation on my soul. Here, you'd sit at the foot of my bed, and thus, would begin your feast! Slowly inching closer and closer. Tearing the sheets that bound me. The gaze of your fiery red glare and abysmal mouth. The razors and knives that began slicing and dicing my body. The blood that splattered—made as a fine wine, so you claimed. The slow fading of life it seemed, yet it was only the beginning. For I was mute—and could not scream. For I was paralyzed—your befouled magics, and bewitching gaze and inflictive haze. Curse you, Incubus! Curse you! How you lied and misled me. How tonight will pass, I shall endure your pain, and one day escape your treacherous way. How you cackle—putrid and profuse with your victory. The darkness in which you bind me, I will survive. For now, I float in darkness. Alone, cold, numb, and decaying.

Temporary salvation blessed am I by the morning's blissful light. I devised a plan. Oh, dear Incubus…it shall soon be your turn. In Death's hour and the prime twilight of darkness. The lights are silhouetted by the shadows of the deceased. The damned cry. The damned pray. Oh, Incubus, I see you stare with your hellish glare—salivating, waiting. I see you smile with your smart mouth. How you would laugh when mother would leave the lights on, and even recruited the night's light to your aid.

However, fair Incubus, I would soon splice your newfound ally and crumble it to its renowned daily task. For now, I am disembodied, and your attack is made. Tonight, you and "Flame," together, take excruciating glee in binding me to the grill of hell; charring my body to your hellish chef standards. Maniacally you cackle as you indulge your late-night snack in your newest and latest victory. The damned cry and pray to falsehoods. Your servant now thrives and is nearly ready. My power grows, and with it, your defeat. Can you feel it, Incubus? Soon.

The new dawn breaks, freeing my soul, returning it to my body. I prepare for the day—self-preservation and honing of my otherworldly skills—I train for the night. For tonight, I would make my stand against your tyranny! So callous are you—casual, in your observance; your grin turned to a sadistic demonic glee. Alas, you wait for the night to come.

My disembodiment approaches, here and where you thought I was unable to resist. Oh, ho ho! How wrong you are Incubus! For as you can see, I have control, dexterity, grace,

and agility, with the savage ferocity of pure will. You...poor
fool. I fend you off until the Light's Salvation, 'twas all I
needed. Yes, for I have aligned myself with the Light. I wonder,
can you now feel the fear you've inflicted upon?

And so, it begins, fair Incubus, the fight that was destined to
be. For I shall be victorious! I shall end your suffering to the
people! For light cannot exist without darkness, I shall take the
place, and with it, your power! Ah, glorious Incubus! Oh, how
your stunned expression did linger.

A new day begins and with it does dawn break. For later in
twilight's eve, shall we face in battle, comrade. Training
continuously, self-empowerment, while deep within did the
seeds of darkness grow—salivating, insatiable, the hunger for
power! Here, you grinned—bastard! You knew you would win.
Fool, for this, shall be the final time! You evolved...dear
friend—a flash of metamorphosis, bestowing upon you more
teeth than a great white, stealth, and the agile reflexes of a
serpent. You hiss and lunge at me, devouring me wholly for the
last time.

As I laid in your disgusting gut, I listened to the cries of the
damned and the demonic prayers that bellowed in your gastric
abyss. Hear me, for I laugh at your wretched being and cry
vengeance, justice, that I shall prevail! That. I. Will. Prevail.
For I, shall be the successor, and you...you shall be the one
devoured. For you see, I shall be the hunter, and you shall be
the prey.

The Light's Grace calls and summons me home—renewed
and whole. I awake and endure my training for the epic battle

of celestial proportions. You will not, however, see me until combat, old friend. Fair Incubus, can you smell it? The approaching scent of defeat? That is the smell of your death that now emanates from you.

Mid-day is now upon us. How you stare, anxiously waiting, hungry, wanting. You wonder…where is your servant? What sort of trickery could he be up to? My old friend and teacher, the final twilight hour has come, and with it, your end. For I shall sleep a valorous knight's sleep, and be ready for battle.

The ancient being, Time, enslaves us both. With haste, you lunge for my soul. The damned dare pray, they dare cry. Do you hear, Incubus? They demand your demise! Relentless is your assault, as my nimble body dodges and endures damage. I try to escape through the door, yet, you had so cleverly bound it with us. Leaving only the window of truth. I make haste for it, but you knew this already. Rigorous is your charge, sending us to the depths out beneath the window—snapping at me on our downfall. I, however, have gained the upper hand and crushed you beneath me.

Wounded, I at last stand victorious. I know you—how you play possum, you dare ploy me, Incubus. I reach for a stone of relinquishment. Raised high to the heavens, as you ready your final attack. I break the rock upon your mouth, not with the hopes of slaying you, but assimilating you. Your attack dazes me into the wall, and already you motion your next move. Here you hope to finish me off and harvest my soul once and for all. I search my being and find that Light's Grace has blessed me the dagger of truth. I raise and find it true to your body—stabbing and cutting your wooden mold.

Hereafter, I set you ablaze in the depths of Hell. For I am victorious. Your wicked gleeful grin decimated and brought to ash. Oh, Incubus, how does the pain of death, defeat and the torment of the damned feel?

The Light's Grace has returned me too early. You linger still, Incubus, I can sense it. Tis a job left unfinished. Where are you?! The damned do not pray. The damned do not cry! They dare not say…where you are. It is unfortunate, but I must now wait for night's newest duel.

The lion's roar rolls across the heavens. The world blinks many at once a time and sheds its impurities on high that fall. The torrential flow of the heavens ushers in the finale of Light versus Dark. Mother Nature dances to the tribal ritual, to the sound—light sets thin and twitches, its spasms ever so often.

For this would be a turn, Incubus you have returned. You have been blessed with the agility and strength of the Gators bite. The swooning love of Pepe Le Pu, you stalk in solitude. For this night, you are to exact vengeance, old friend. Yes, tonight, there would not be any mistakes. You come to me above as I slumber. The very tool of my salvation and my freedom is now the instrument of exact vengeance, fear, and destruction. You smile as you gaze, cackling, taunting, gesturing at me, hinting my demise. Here, you crash through my window and pull me by the throat out. You devour me yet again Incubus—consuming my body bit by bit. You cackle manically as you drink my blood as your wine. My short-lived victory—and the Light's betrayal. I will have my revenge—on them both! Yes, Incubus, your end will be soon.

So, you have come, my friend, no doubt to quench your thirst and hunger. I give unto you to satisfy: my anger, hatred, misery, and torment! It is here, where you pull me through the window yet again. Our fate—entwined—as we collapse together onto the ground. Broken and battered are you; I raise your Light blessed, one-half of righteousness to quell your rampage for me. You lacerate—attempting to dismember and disfigure my being. I counter with hacking and slashing at your slender, and beautiful form. It is here…here where your soul is spilled upon the ground. The damned are finally freed and pour out from your gut. The Light will not save you, old friend. I reach for your soul and devour it wholly. For I was once merciful, just and pure, I grant you a cruel death—in part all the more suffering unto you. I confine and bind you, and while you are tortured, bound, and forced upon an eternity of those you took—their vengeance exacted and complete.

The Light finally arrives—disembodied spirit reclaims the body, rejuvenating the broken body and assimilates you, Incubus. You are defeated. However, I know you…one day, you will break free. For you will return, and again attempt. Yet, I shall be waiting—salivating, insatiable and wanting. Oh, Incubus. How I have become…you.

The Strange Man at the Bar

A LONE MAN SAT ON a bar stool, hunched over, face flat out against the cool of the polished, hardwood bar counter top. He pushed himself up, erecting and straightening his back. He rolled his head from side to side, and front to back. His sleep-deprived eyes focused on the environment that bewildered him.

Where did everyone go to?

He scanned the room for a soul, but only found that he was the sole survivor. He stood up and backed away from the counter to gaze out into the street, where pure darkness settled around. The bar was dull and dim lit—almost as if lit by a lone match that had been struck. Albeit, there was a spark of life who occupied within the walls. The doors were barricaded—

chained and bound, letting nothing in...and surely nothing out. The man pondered and scratched his head, he was lost in the most puzzling ordeal he found himself in.

There were but three, plus the bartender and me. Now how can it be that all that is left...is me? Why have they gone, where to? How did the doors entwine so with chains, locks, and such complexity that I am bound here? Surely, this is a joke? Ah, yes, they must all be in the back laughing it up—playing tricks on such a drunken fool, such shenanigans!

The man shuffled his way to the back of the bar, where the door opened to the kitchen, but there was not a soul—only the hum of the electrifying air that buzzed with an unfashionable spectacle. The sounds startled the man and caused him to jump. He retreated from the forsaken kitchen. As he retraced his steps, a repetitive thud, began to echo into the lounge.

It is nothing. I saw nothing, be it nothing, for it is nothing. Perhaps it is a mouse? Maybe the refrigerator is broken? Be it the freezer thawing? Whatever it may be, it is of no concern. It is nothing.

The man shrugged as he turned full circle and found his home from once where he had awakened. He made himself comfortable, but his mouth beckoned him—dry. He licked his lips and smacked them once, wiping them with his right hand.

He sighed and looked about, thereby deciding that if indeed a trick was in progress, he would wager a prize. "I shall take a drink then. 'On the house' you say? You are too kind. I shall take my pick!" The man looked around the bar once again and stood up. He looked behind the bar and reached for a glass, and a rustic, dusted over, bottle of bourbon. "Yes, this will do quite well, thank you." He unscrewed the top and poured himself a glassful, and sat the bottle down...close. He raised his newfound elixir to his lips and washed his once parched hunger away.

Satisfied, the man returned the glass to the counter and brought his hand to the bottle of bourbon. "Hello, old friend, how are you today? How is the missus and of Jim, Tim, and Mary? Ah, yes such a fine family you have." He smiled as he conversed. Clearly, the bottle made no explicit remark but gave a bow. He rose his glass to his friend and as like before it, met the same fate. Again, he returned the glass, and looked on, across the bar at the mirror that gazed back at the man.

A long brown overcoat, ebony suit and long crimson tie, a mild-mannered dressed man sat reverse opposite. He was clean shaven and moderately aged, with a few hoary hairs sprouting from the well-kept beard and hair. A few wrinkles told of a hard worker and overstressed individual. Pallid blue-gray eyes matched the color of his button-down shirt. He ran his red right hand over his face, top to bottom, letting a sigh escape. Before returning his red right hand to the bottle, he further greeted it and praised its kindness. He thanked it once more by toasting to life.

He caught an eye of the clock that crawled on the wall as if it were a spider weaving its web. The hands both stopped on six. He remarked at the coincidence that it made, noting that it was a shame that there was no second hand to mark the possibility of a third six. He let loose a chuckle and furthered his indulgence of his refreshment.

While he did so, the echo of the thud from the kitchen had subsided, only to begin a soft whisper in his ear. Pain shot through his head, eye to eye and to the top to bottom of his head. He clenched the bar in pain. It was so agonizing, he nearly dropped to the floor. However, it subsided, and the whisper became clearer, like that of a moan. A light cackle, bone cracking, sight of blood gushing, and the taste of dirt overtook his senses.

What tomfoolery is this!? What manner of a trick do you play on me!?

The mirror that sat across from him now sat before him. He looked to his only friend, but only found a corpse. "My dear friend, what has happened to you? Where is your head? Where is your body? You have nearly dried up!"

The room stifled and began to warm beyond reasonable conditions as if the heat was turned to max or if perhaps inside in a dry, dusty mouth. A set pattern of thuds began to overtake within the room, leaving the man to search for a cause and deliver a rational, soluble explanation.

Perhaps the boiler is broken, or the controls have become dysfunctional. It must be another trick!

For then and there, there did mutter a low raspy voice, spoken from the other side (or was it that it seemed to come from within the room?). "It is no trick, sir. Everything is as it is. You are alone. You have been abandoned. You have betrayed your best friend. You have been captured, as time has deemed it so, your hourglass is at an end. The time for atonement has come. Your custodial precedence has come to pass...Relinquish from the flesh, from the taint you carry..."

For then the large mirror grew large veins and pulsated with life. The wall chafed and flaked onto the floor. The beating of a pulse—of a heart—of life who echoed throughout the vast room. An eye emerged from within the mirror. The mirrored image of the man grinned malevolently as it stood in the amber of the great eye. As then there was a maniacal cackle that was let loose, and the horror that betook the man's breath as his image was dismembered from many lucid dark, razor-edged tentacles. They tore the legs off, then the arms—ripping the organs as if some wild pack of hounds tearing into a fresh kill. Then finally there went the head—the image laughed maniacally, while the eyes popped and gushed blood from the eye sockets, mouth, and nose. The protrusion of the tentacles through the eye sockets, where the pieces of the image's body fell into the pupil of the eyes' darkness.

For next, the stools came to life, much like the tentacles that tore his reflection. Terrified, he fended against one that writhed its way to him, trying to encase itself around his legs. "I will not be taken! I will not let a mind trick on a drunken fool consume me! I shall prevail!" The man yelled as he stomped the tentacle off.

The excellent amber cat's eye fixated, and a growl shook the room as then a tentacle fashioned itself a blade, as if a hacksaw, gnawing its way into the man's arm. As the man screamed with pain, a familiar voice boomed from within,

"You think this still a trick, a play on sobriety, dear sir? No, you feel what you do, know this as it is all...far...too real." The man panicked and let loose cries for help, as the voice cackled with joy, "No one is coming to save you. Nothing can and nothing will." As the man pleaded for life over death and wrestled with the monstrosities that sought to leech his life, he contemplated a plan. Even if he were to fail, he believed that if at least he tried, he would have no regrets in falling to the beast who laid siege on his life.

The man scrambled to his feet and grabbed his friend's body, and hurled it at the tentacle that attacked him. The contents smashed and dazed the beast all but momentarily, clearly angering it further. He reached for a lighter and flicked the flint until it lit. He tossed it at the creature causing it to be set ablaze. Agonizing were the cries that were heard from within the room. The eye grew clearly angered, and more tentacles sought after the man. He grabbed a chair and hurled it at the mirror causing it chip and break—blood squirted and sprayed across the room. "What are you doing to me?! You are but a fool in your poor attempts to foil me! You delay only the inevitable!"

He continued relentlessly smashing at the mirror, as the vast eye slowly became dissolved, and littered the floor. The tentacles lunged for the man, knocking him across the room. He steadily rose to his feet, his hand pressed against the wall, he could feel the warmth and the pulsation that could be perceived throughout. He retracted his hand and searched for something to further his assault, finding only a fork and knife.

He jabbed the utensils into the wall, as shrieks were heard, the door that had led to the kitchen manifested into the fashion of a mouth, with razor sharp teeth and enough force to crush the mightiest of steel. The tentacles flailed and sought after the man, who frantically rushed to be out of reach from the limbs, and mouth. He grabbed a chair and tried to smash the window that had looked outside, but only bore more darkness. The window held sound, and soon an eye manifested upon the glass pane.

There is no hope, nothing I can do any longer. I have done all that I can. I have no regrets. I have nothing that will worry me any further. I have lived what I have and will hold out for as long as I am able to before the end comes for me.

The man closed his eyes as he held off the attacks made upon him. Try as he did, he was no match for the overwhelming power that surrounded him. The tentacles enveloped him and dragged him to the kitchen door, where the beast began to tear him limb from limb. His torso delved into by the serrated blades of the tentacles that came from the darkness. Then his head rushed with the momentous pain of his eyes bursting from his skull. He laughed maniacally as the mirror image had come to pass, despite his efforts to change his future. As the darkness encompassed him, he felt the constant pain, even though his body was completely dismembered. Within the blackness, would come the reality of it all.

The man shot up straight from his bar stool, nearly toppling over. The bartender eyed him carefully and with a raised eyebrow. Searching around, he counted but three, plus he and the barkeep. He looked towards the kitchen and saw a light. A bottle sat empty next to him, and a glass...not half empty or full. A smile crawled across his face, and at once when he peered towards the door and saw it was bright and free. The window lit by the streetlights that waltzed in the cold early morning.

He sighed with relief and called the barkeep over. "My tab if you will be it paid in full." The barkeep nodded and tallied up the bill, while the man looked to the empty bottle and small bottle of sleeping pills. "Thank you, my old friend. You've shown me a deal; next time I will not be a meal. Thank you, thank you, thank you!"

As the barkeep returned and handed the bill, the man overpaid and wished a good night. He waved to the others and went to the door. Before exiting, he looked up above the bar to the time.

3:33?

He turned and pushed the door with his red right hand, and wandered out into the desolate night, laughing to himself with renewed vigor.

Who? Me?

I T WAS A DARK and chilly night. The kind where the stars littered the sky with their brilliance. The wind was absent while the air was chilled from the rain some time ago.

A man stirred within a home, set in the middle of a street. He was restless and parched. He cautiously made his way into the kitchen in the dark. He stopped before the fridge and rubbed his young green eyes; fatigue had long been set. He scratched the back of his scalp, the mess of blond hair peeked through the cracks of his fingertips.

Man, I'm so tired, he thought. *I really hope they're late picking us up. I've barely had any sleep.* The man thought to himself as he let out a muffled yawn.

He reached into the fridge, the light blinding him temporarily, searching for a bottle of whiskey. His pale hand finally caught reminiscence of the bottle marked with "Jack

Daniels." He grinned to himself as he found his friend and confidant.

He then heard a creak outside, on what he believed to be the deck to the backyard. He chuckled to himself as he was so easily startled.

Probably an animal again, he thought.

As gravity maintained its order, closing the fridge door behind the man, he walked across the kitchen into the living room. His silhouette elongated his tall figure above the wall and ceiling. He picked up the empty glass on the dark oval coffee table, then retreated to the kitchen. He then heard another creak...this time on the front porch.

Okay, that's a little too freaky...hmm.

The man put the glass and bottle of whiskey down on the kitchen countertop, and walked cautiously to the front window and peered out into the night. Nothing... He saw nothing on the doorstep, nor in view, but the street and neighbors' lights. He shrugged it off and went back to the counter where his drink sat...waiting.

He poured a glassful and began drinking the contents immediately. He looked down at the bottle of empty pills. Shortly after that, he heard an ominous creaking on the deck again, followed by a tapping on the window. The tapping increased exponentially, causing him to grow fearful.

It all seemed too coincidental.

What the hell?

He reached for his handgun and a hunting knife that was stored high above in a kitchen cabinet. Slowly, he crept towards the back door, passing the laundry, and bathroom…the path lit only by sporadic nightlights. He approached the back door, and cautiously unlocked the door. He opened it and found…nothing. Nothing but the twilight greeted him, the fresh air rushing against his warm face. He closed the door and locked it tight, just as he had found it, and withdrew his weapons. He stumbled back through the house, where he had heard the tapping on the window. He pulled back the curtains…nothing. Nothing was there but the night.

I must be exhausted…or maybe it's the pills.

He smirked, and let out another deep yawn.

He walked through the living room, and made way to his daughter's, and his wife's bedrooms…both slept soundly. As he went to go check on his daughter again, only to just turn a light off, he heard the same haunting sounds…

This time, he went to the window of his daughter's room and drew back the curtains. To his horror, several groups of eyes fixated upon him—twitching, blinking, glaring—with more slowly populating outside the window pane.

He closed the curtains with haste…masking whatever was out there. The tapping then evolved into scraping…not only at the windows but at the doors all over the house—the sound was becoming louder with every passing moment. The young man scooped up his slumbering daughter and rushed her to his and his wife's room. He urgently woke her and told her what events were taking place outside, and to call 911.

As his wife reached for the telephone and dialed, there was only static, and a mocking laughter that could be heard on the other end of the line. She even tried with the cell phone, only to find it yielding the same results. The laughter began to whisper...

"No—o one ca—n s—ave you."

She dropped the phone on the ground as it cackled maniacally back at their apparent impending doom. Here they found themselves alone...trapped. The scraping and tapping became louder...near deafening and more forceful. The man feared for his family, for whatever was outside, wanting to try and get in, would surely kill them all unmercifully.

The thought became apparent to him then. If I'm going to die...I'm going to die defending them.

The young man readied his weapons, as he took a final glance back at his horrified wife and still slumbering child, "Stay here!"

He made his way to his daughter's window and slid it open. He slashed wildly and blindly at whatever was outside the window. There was a loud shriek, followed by a thud on the pavement. The man then shut the window and rushed to the front door. He took a breath and then quickly unlocked the front door, and fired a few shots from his handgun out into the night. Screams of again were heard, followed by a tremendous weight that was sent crashing to the ground. The man closed the door and bolted it shut.

After several moments, the haunting ended... The man mustered the courage to open the door, to see just what it was that was plaguing him and his family at this hour. The horror of his life came to pass as to what he found on his doorstep.

There laid the familiar silhouette of a man…a shot to the chest, and two bullets in his head. In his arms, the man cradled a small girl who, by the looks, had seized up…and a hole that bored through her little head into the man's heart. Both laid dead in a bloody mess. The young man ran out and checked the side of his house where his daughter's window shared with the driveway. He found another familiar silhouette…this one of a woman—dead—her body slashed up, and her throat slit. In her hand, she held a small pebble, bloodied from her own blood.

The man panicked at the sight before his eyes and rushed back towards the entrance of his house. Out front, there was a red sedan—the insides were torn, battered, and smashed to hell. He stumbled through the darkness, back into his home to tell his wife of what he found. He entered his home and made his way to see his wife and daughter—both dead… His wife's throat was slit while his daughter laid with a hole in her small head.

No…No…N—no, no, no, no!

His eyes widened, and he collapsed to his knees at his bedside.

Did…did…did I? No—no…I.

He then rushed to his daughter's room and gazed out the dim night where the familiar woman laid. He found…nothing. He ran back to his wife and daughter. The door to the bedroom was now closed…whereas…when he left it, it was open.

Slowly, he tapped on the door and motioned to open the door. The door flung open, the darkness inside it wholly… Gunfire erupted from within it. Here, at the doorway, he collapsed. Darkness grew around him, as did the cold that soaked him to the marrow and through. As the frigid darkness embraced him and took him in, he felt life escape him entirely.

He shot up from the stool in the kitchen. Another nightmare... He moved the empty glass and bottle on the counter, next to the now empty bottle of anti-depressant and sleeping pills. He shuffled his way back to the bedroom where his wife and daughter once laid. The door slowly closed behind him. The sound of a "click" was heard...like that of a hammer on a handgun. All there was...was sobbing...and then silence.

Outside, a white van had arrived and honked its horn. The driver hopped out and went to knock on the door, only to find it ajar. He opened it up to see no one at first. He yelled out if anyone was home, but just found silence. He wandered to the bedroom, where he knew the man slept. He opened the door to see the man in bed...alone...dead, with a bullet hole in his head.

Acknowledgements

Thanks to my wife for putting up with my shenanigans. You're amazing. We should go on a vacation. Like Europe?

My kids for being crazy and a chunk off the old blocks.

I would like to thank the members of Morphine and all associated friends. Thank you for all the wonderful music you guys have produced and to Mark Sandman [Rest in Peace].

Thanks to Buckethead.

Thanks to my friends for your continued support.

The staff at the Okemos, MI Old Chicago. You guys rock!

My *World of Warcraft* friends on the US server Aegwynn, and in the Horde guild, Revolt. You're all demoted to 'Used Tampon.'

With love,

Sin

Anyone else I may have forgotten to mention...thank you.

About the Author

Robert J. S. T. McCartney loves to write about the strange and bizarre. The urban fantasy novel *Lilah's Guide to Hoyle* was written in collaboration with his friend and co-author, Albert Debusschere III. He currently lives in Knoxville, Tennessee with his wife and kids.

He is the author of the *Among Us: Contact, Assimilation, Control, Extermination Series*, *The Chronicles of Bob: The Chronic Suicidal*, *Abnormal Side Effects*, and other stories.

He also plays *World of Warcraft* and loves some sweet tunes.

Visit us at www.abnormalpublishing.com for more stories.